Rosamond du Jardin

BOY TROUBLE

By the same author

MARCY CATCHES UP

DOUBLE DATE

CLASS RING

WAIT FOR MARCY

PRACTICALLY SEVENTEEN

Boy Trouble

A TOBEY HEYDON STORY

by

Rosamond du Jardin

J. B. LIPPINCOTT COMPANY
PHILADELPHIA AND NEW YORK

PRINTED IN THE UNITED STATES OF AMERICA

FIRST EDITION

Library of Congress Catalog Card Number 53-5423

Contents

BOY TROUBLE

1

Of time and the prom

If there is a more exciting time in a girl's life than the one when she's up to her ears in the senior prom and her graduation from high school, it certainly hasn't happened to me yet. Sometimes lately I've had the queerest sensation, a sort of burning wish that I could make time slow down for a while and let me go on living this particular period indefinitely. When I remarked about this desire of mine the other night at the dinner table, my family came up with some very mixed reactions.

My younger sister, Midge, who is ten and sandy-haired and the only one of my three sisters left at home, the older two being married, exclaimed, "Phoo on that!"

"Why?" I asked dreamily. "Just think, there'll be the prom in two weeks, then graduation and all. I'm having such a lush time!"

"I'm not," Midge stated flatly. "Creeps, I can't wait till school's out! If it wasn't for vacation being just three weeks and one day off, I'd die."

My father chuckled. "Haven't you got it figured out in hours yet? Or minutes?"

Dad has gray hair and is sort of thinnish, quite well preserved really for a man in his later forties. His sense of humor has survived four daughters and being the only male in the Heydon household for years and years, so it must have been a dilly to start with. My mother is quite good humored, too, and very nice looking in a mature way. She can still get into a size sixteen, which seems to give her a good deal of satisfaction. It makes me happy, too, because I am able to borrow her jackets, although her skirts are miles too big for me.

"That'd take arithmetic," Midge informed my father coldly. "And I get enough of that cruddy subject from ol' Miss Carson, so I don't do any of it on my own time."

She bit morosely into her hot roll, on which she had loaded so much jam it was practically dripping. My sister's table manners are pretty revolting, but when I looked at Mom to see if she wasn't going to speak to her, Mom was staring sort of vaguely into space, as if she were deep in thought.

After a minute she spoke, but not about the strawberries beginning to dribble down over Midge's fingers. Mom said, "It would be nice if a person could simply stretch time out like a rubber band. Then, when you were enjoying yourself, you could make it last and last. And when you weren't, you could let time snap back and have your misery over in a hurry."

My father shook his head. "Wouldn't do at all. I see all kinds of complications. Tobey'd be stretching these weeks out and Midge would be letting them snap together. And you and I would be worn to a frazzle trying to remember that what was today for Tobey would be three weeks or so from now for Midge."

"That's right," Mom laughed across the table at him. "It wouldn't work. I guess we'd better leave time alone."

"I read a story once," my father said thoughtfully. "I think H. G. Wells wrote it. All about a man who invented some kind of a machine that would take him backward or forward in time. And he could stop and stay a while in any period he wanted to, see how it was and all. Quite a fascinating idea."

"You mean," Mom asked, "we could go back to our teens again?" She didn't sound too enthusiastic.

"That," Dad said, "would be a mere trifle for Mr. Wells's machine. We could go back into prehistoric times or forward into the fortieth century."

Midge exclaimed, her eyes shining, "Or I could be a cowboy back in the Old West, when there were horses running wild all over the range."

My little sister is loopy about horses. If she got really started on the subject, there'd be no stopping her.

I broke in, wishing I'd never brought up the question of time at all, "Can't we have dessert now, Mom? Brose is coming over at seven."

Mom said, "Why, yes, dear. I guess everyone's finished." She noticed Midge licking her fingers then and frowned. "Midge, please! Must you eat like a little animal?"

"Huh-uh," Midge said. "But it's fun."

"Not for the rest of us," I informed her, getting up to help Mom carry out dishes and bring in the dessert.

It proved to be chocolate cake, which is a favorite around our house. We all fell to with good appetite and it wasn't until Dad's generous slice was more than half gone that he looked up at me to inquire in a slightly accusing tone, "Did I understand you to say Brose is coming over tonight—again?"

I nodded.

"Brose Gilman," my father went on aggrievedly, "spends considerably more time here than he does under his own roof. It's not that I dislike him, but can't he stay home one night a week? Doesn't he owe that much to his parents?"

I sighed. "Honestly, Dad! You know he's not here every night."

"Seems like it to me," Dad insisted. "Monday night I'm sure he was here. And Tuesday and Wednesday and now Thursday." He glanced at Mom for corroboration.

But I corrected quickly, "Not Tuesday, Dad. That was the night I did my hair and went to bed real early."

"Brose was sick then?" my father inquired with utmost gravity. "I'm sure he wouldn't have deprived us of the pleasure of his company for any less vital reason."

"It does seem," Mom put in plaintively, "as if we've seen more than usual of him lately. I rather thought, now that you aren't wearing his class ring—"

"But we're still just as good friends as ever," I told her. "We haven't broken up or anything. It's just that wearing each other's class rings—well, it seems a little juvenile now that we're almost eighteen."

My father choked slightly and I knew it was because he found my statement funny. I gave him a cool look.

I had explained all this to Mom and him before, there was really no point in going into the whole business in detail again. But parents can be so dense sometimes, even nice up-to-date parents like mine. I had worn Brose Gilman's ring almost all of our senior year. But after our most recent quarrel, even though we had made up again, I wouldn't take his ring back. It hadn't been easy for him to understand my feelings in the matter, but I'd made them clear finally. Brose saw, as I did, that we could be just as good friends, just as fond of each other, without swapping rings. When you're practically old enough to go to college, wearing a boy's ring seems sort of pointless. Next fall we'd be apart, going to different schools, writing each other, of course, but dating other people. Still, fall was several months off yet. And the fact that we weren't wearing each other's rings any longer didn't mean that we liked each other any less, or didn't want to spend all the time we could together.

Mom said approvingly, "I think it's very smart of you, dear, to see that. But the thing I don't understand is why you and Brose spend so much time at home lately. I mean, he used to take you out more, to the movies and all."

"Now they'd just rather sit and hold hands," Midge said in one of her more sickening tones, "and kiss when they think nobody's looking."

I gave her a poisonous look. "That's not so! And anyway, what have you been doing, hiding in the woodwork?" I turned my attention back to my parents. "The thing is," I informed them, "Brose and I are staying home lately for two good reasons. One is I'm helping him with his French. He's very shaky in it and he's just got to pass his exam because he needs the credits in order to graduate."

"Of course," Mom nodded sympathetically. "It's nice of you to help him, too."

"He'll make it all right—I think," I told her. "If he can just get irregular verbs through his thick head. Of course, he helps me with math. That's my worst subject."

"Isn't it lucky," Dad asked, "that you both aren't weak in the same thing? That would probably put an end to a beautiful romance."

I ignored him. There are times when there is nothing else you can do with my father.

Midge asked, "What's the other reason you aren't going out so much any more? You said there were two, Tobey."

"If you must know," I told her, "it's because we're saving Brose's money for the prom."

"Oh," Midge inquired with the unthinking ignorance of childhood, "is it expensive?"

"Is it!" I said with feeling. "You have no idea!"

Our prom was being held at the country club, as usual, but the band committee had let itself get carried away a little on the music. As a result the tickets cost more than they had for any other school dance I could remember. Besides, Brose would have my corsage to buy and all the other incidentals that went into a big evening. It had become a sort of tradition at Edgewood High to stay out very late on prom night. This usually entailed driving in to Chicago after the dance, a distance of some twenty-five miles, and going to one of the big hotel night clubs. All in all the prom was an expensive proposition for a boy and the least his girl could do was co-operate in helping him save on dates in advance.

By the time I had made all this clear to Midge and my parents, it was almost seven. Luckily, it was Midge's turn to help Mom with the dishes. I could hear her moaning and groaning about it all the way upstairs as I went to get ready.

I didn't have to change my clothes. The white turtleneck sweater and plaid skirt I was wearing would do, since we were only going to work on Brose's French assignment and take a walk afterward. I had it all figured out that we'd have a snack from the refrigerator, instead of stopping for sodas at Joe's Grill, which is our favorite hangout. We were really going to have to pinch Brose's pennies hard to afford the prom. But having heard the griping going on around school lately, I knew we weren't the only ones feeling the financial squeeze. Lots of others were even worse off than we.

I brushed my hair, which is a sort of coppery color that goes well with my brown eyes, and tied it in a pony tail with a black ribbon. I like my hair that way and Brose has finally got used to it so he likes it, too. Men are sort of hard to jolt out of their familiar rut sometimes. It's a good thing they have women around to work on them or they'd never get used to new fashions. I leaned a little nearer the mirror to see whether the freckles on my nose showed. They are getting less noticeable as I grow older, thank goodness. Brose claims he likes them, anyway. He is very sweet at times. Of course, there are other times when he isn't, but I guess all men are like that and you just have to take them as they are.

By the time I had put on fresh lipstick and fixed my nail polish where it was a little chipped, I could hear Brose downstairs talking with my father. They get along so well, I didn't feel I had to hurry. Brose is used to waiting for me, although I never overdo it and try his patience too far. But I don't consider it smart to let a man think you're too anxious and just hanging at the window watching and waiting for him to arrive.

When I went down, it couldn't have been more than seven-twenty and Brose and my father were in the library. They were sitting and talking as they usually do, but Brose looked up as I came in and there was the most annoyed scowl on his face.

"Gee whiz, Tobey," he demanded before I could even say a word, "can't you ever be ready when I get here?"

My mouth dropped open a little in surprise. It wasn't like Brose to be so grumpy. He got to his feet and I stood there staring blankly at him. Even frowning, he is quite nice looking, big and with broad shoulders and dark hair and eyes. He had his French book in one hand and he sort of tapped it against his leg, as if he were under some kind of tension. I couldn't imagine what was wrong with him, because generally he is very easygoing and good natured.

"Well, that's a nice greeting, I must say!" I snapped right back at him.

My father opened his mouth as if to speak and then shut it again, apparently having thought better of it. One thing you can say for Dad, his sense of humor may be a bit corny, but at least he knows when to keep it under control. And evidently he realized that this was no time for kidding.

Brose had the grace to look a little sorry. "I didn't mean to bark at you," he apologized, "but—" he broke off and I had the queerest feeling that his eyes were actually pleading with me.

"Is it your French?" I asked. "Because if that's what you're worried about, we can get at it right away."

But Brose shook his head and a lock of hair fell forward across his forehead, making him look about seven years old, so that my heart actually twisted in sympathy. He gulped, "It's not that. In fact—well, I was wondering if maybe we couldn't go out for a walk first, Tobey, and do my assignment later."

His eyes still clung to mine desperately, so that I realized there was something he wanted to tell me, something private, something that couldn't even wait until after I'd helped him with his French.

"Of course, Brose," I told him.

I grabbed my corduroy jacket out of the hall closet and went out into the lovely spring night with Brose, apprehension nipping at me.

2

Nuts to you!

I DON'T SUPPOSE WE HAD TAKEN MORE than half a dozen steps off our front porch when Brose began to spill out his tale of woe. If it had happened to anyone else, or even to him at some other time, it might have struck me as hilariously funny. After all, I have a strong sense of humor and even now, realizing all the implications of disaster in the situation, I could hardly suppress a mad impulse to burst into laughter as Brose's glum voice recounted his misadventure of that afternoon.

He had gone into Tareyton's drugstore to buy some notebook paper, a legitimate enough errand if there ever was one. If it hadn't happened that I'd gone to a Y-Teens' club meeting after school, I'd no doubt have been with him. It was sheer chance, too, that he had run into Itchy Stearns and Sox Trevor, two of his closest friends, in the after-school throng around the soda fountain and had stopped to talk. I could just see the scene as Brose described it, the kids laughing and yelling at each other as usual, poor Mr. Tareyton hovering about, understandably anxious since his crowded little store had so often been the scene of some accident in the past. Once a showcase had been broken and several times perfume displays had been inadvertently knocked over. Mr. Tareyton didn't really encourage teen-age patronage. It was just his bad luck to be located so conveniently to the high school that he almost had to sell school supplies. Also, he got most of the overflow from Joe's Grill across the street, whether he wanted it or not.

Anyway, there was Brose, innocently gabbing with Sox and Itchy. And right behind him, although he didn't realize it, was the case filled with fresh roasted nuts, all sorts of them, each variety in its own little compartment.

"We weren't really rough-housing like Mr. Tareyton said. Honestly, we weren't," Brose informed me miserably.

I didn't doubt that what he said was true. You take three large eighteen-year-olds and confine them in a small space and you have all the ingredients for disaster whether they get rough or not. One of them is bound to upset something or trip over something or bump something with his elbow.

"Anyway," Brose went on, his tone so low and dejected you could practically scrape it off the sidewalk, "I swear all I did was turn around to go and then there was this darn nut case right in front of me and I couldn't help bumping into it—" he stopped. He really didn't have to say any more.

It was at this point in his story that I felt the mad impulse to giggle. But I restrained it. And almost at once, as Brose got his voice under control again and went on talking, I felt my urge to laugh wither and die as the full enormity of the thing that had happened hit me.

"Nuts," Brose groaned, "all over the place. You never saw so many nuts, Tobey."

"You mean you broke the case?" I gasped.

Brose shook his head. "No, it just sort of came open. That's the only good thing about the whole deal. If I'd had to pay for the case, it'd probably have cost me a mint. As it was—" he gulped, "I just had to buy all those nuts."

I could only stop dead still, right there on the sidewalk, with the moonlight falling in lacy patterns through the trees all around us. I stared up at him. "All of them?"

"Every last nut," Brose said bitterly, "half of 'em spilled all over the floor and absolutely no good. All those fancy, expensive kinds like women eat at bridge parties. Only a few cheap ones like peanuts. You see, the thing was, those that didn't spill on the floor got all mixed up together. So Mr. Tareyton said he couldn't sell 'em, because they're all different prices and nobody would want to pay for pecans and brazil nuts with peanuts mixed in. I didn't want to pay for 'em, either," Brose sort of moaned, "but what else could I do? I couldn't have him going to my father about it."

All those nickels and dimes and dollars we had saved on sodas and movies, that we had been going to squander so gloriously on the prom, spent for nuts.

I asked, appalled, "How much, Brose?"

"Brace yourself," Brose warned. "Eleven dollars and fifty cents. And all I got is maybe a couple of pounds of fancy nuts to show for it. Gosh, Tobey—"

He sounded so miserable I laid my hand over his. I wished I could think of some way to comfort him, but I was feeling so low myself it wasn't easy.

"It's—lucky you've already bought our prom tickets," I finally came up with.

But that didn't help much.

"Yeah," Brose said, "but what about your flowers and going in to the Empire Room afterward? Gosh, Tobey, this has taken such a big bite out of my cash—well, I just can't swing anything but the prom. You'll be lucky to get some little dinky corsage instead of an orchid like I'd planned."

I squeezed his hand harder. "I don't care, Brose. I don't care a bit." It wasn't true, but I couldn't bear having him so unhappy. I rushed on, "The corsage isn't the really important thing about the prom. And neither's a night club afterward." My voice didn't come out quite so convincing as I meant it to. But anyway, I tried.

Brose said huskily, "Gee, Tobey. It's swell of you to take it like this. Some girls would have hit the ceiling, blamed me for being a big clumsy oaf."

"No, they wouldn't," I argued, impelled to defend my sex. "Anyone can have an accident. It's just unlucky yours happened to be so expensive."

"I told my dad about it," Brose went on. "I sort of hoped maybe he'd offer to help me out. But he didn't. He and Mom are still kind of sore, I guess, over that lamp I tipped over and broke last week. All I got was a lecture from them on being more careful. Of course, I guess maybe they figure, too, that after giving me a tux and all for my birthday, that's as far as they'll help me out with the prom."

"I don't suppose you can really blame them," I had to admit. After all, Brose's parents were going to be putting out a lot of money to send him to college next fall. He was going to study engineering at Colorado. I was merely going to Central, which isn't much more than commuting distance from Edgewood, but my parents were a little worried about where the money was coming from to cover my expenses. What with taxes and the high cost of living these days, nobody seems to have as much as they used to. I added, to comfort Brose still further, "After all, we're not the only ones who can't afford all the prom trimmings. You should have heard the griping going on at Y-Teens this afternoon."

"Yeah, I know," Brose agreed, sounding maybe a shade more cheerful at the realization of others being in the same boat. "A lot of guys I know aren't even asking a girl to the prom. They claim they can't swing it, with the tickets costing five bucks a couple and then all the stuff a girl expects besides."

I nodded as we walked on along the street, cozily arm in arm. "Seems to me proms have sort of got out of hand these last few years anyway. Why, Mom and Dad were saying that when they were in high school, the prom was just held in the gym. And nobody thought of staying out till three or four o'clock in the morning at some night spot. In fact," I admitted, "I was having an awful time persuading them it was okay for us to stay out that late. Even when I told them practically everyone did, they didn't like it. I expect they'll be just as happy you can't afford it now."

"You're disappointed, though, aren't you, Tobey?" Brose pressed. "I knew you would be—but, gee—"

"At least, I've got a date for the prom," I said as staunchly as I could. "Lots of the girls today were scared stiff nobody was going to ask them. And some of the others were just so hopeless, they're reconciled to their fate. It seems a shame, really. You look forward to the senior prom during all your four years of school. And then, not to be asked—well, it just seems brutal."

"Yeah, but the girls have themselves to blame," Brose argued. "They get all starry-eyed over the prom and want more than a guy can afford. So he clams up and doesn't ask 'em at all. Then they gripe about it."

"I suppose so," I sighed.

"Y'darn right," Brose said, warming to his subject. "Why, just look how much the prom really sets a guy back. The tickets, the corsage, the cost of renting formal clothes if he hasn't got any and a lot of 'em haven't. And then," he paused for effect, "a supper club. Brother, the girl who first dreamed up that idea as a climax to the prom really loused things up."

"How do you know it was a girl?" I demanded. "Probably some boy thought of it, to impress his date with what a big wheel he was."

"No guy's got that big a hole in his head," Brose insisted. "Besides the money involved, you got to talk your folks into letting you use the car, or double date with some other couple who has transportation. And you have to persuade your parents that it's okay to stay out till all hours, that everyone else is doing it, too, on prom night. Why, man, I'll bet all together a fella spends twenty-five bucks or more on the prom, besides the arguing and explaining he has to do to work out all the angles. No wonder lots of 'em aren't going."

I sighed. "There's no use getting all steamed up over it, I suppose. We aren't going to spend any twenty-five bucks. You haven't got it."

It wasn't really very nice of me to remind him. He deflated just like a balloon when somebody lets the air out of it.

"Yeah, that's right," he said glumly. "What am I sounding off about?"

"I'm sorry," I told him. "You'll see, we'll have a real swell time. We'll get to go to the prom, that's the main event anyway. If you'd heard the girls weeping and wailing this afternoon, you'd have known how many of them would be more than happy just to settle for the prom, without any of the trimmings thrown in."

"Yeah?" Brose asked in surprise. "Too bad they don't let the fellas in on the secret. Maybe more of 'em would get asked then. But a guy doesn't like to look cheap and he figures there are just certain things a girl expects on a prom date."

An idea was beginning to form in my head. I didn't say anything while we walked maybe a half block. I was thinking. Here were the girls, maybe close to half of the girls I knew, who weren't going to get to go to the prom after looking forward to it for four years. Here were the boys, who must have looked forward to the prom, too, but who couldn't afford to invite a girl because the occasion had come to include so many expensive side issues. It looked from where I sat like a vicious circle. It looked as if somebody should do something about it.

I said as much to Brose.

"Yeah?" his tone was lackadaisical. "What, for instance?"

"Where's your sense of leadership?" I demanded. "We ought to think of something. After all, we're in the same boat, except you have asked me to the prom and don't think I'd let you out of it."

"I don't want to get out," Brose assured me earnestly, "so long as you won't mind missing all the stuff afterward."

"How about—" I was still thinking hard, "I've got it! Why couldn't a bunch of us girls organize some parties at home for after the prom? Lots of us have rumpus rooms or big living rooms like ours. We could call them different night clubs, maybe fix 'em up a little. It would be practically as much fun as chasing in to the city. And think how much cheaper it would be. What do you think, Brose?"

"The fellas would sure go for it," he said approvingly. "But do you think the girls would? And how would you broadcast all this?"

"It shouldn't be too hard," I said, warming to the idea. "After all, we've got two weeks. First thing tomorrow, I'll circulate a petition among the senior girls. I can just see it now! Something like, 'We, the undersigned, do hereby solemnly pledge that we will not go to a supper club after the prom, that a date with any one of us involves just the dance and whatever form of free entertainment afterward that can be supplied by parties at various homes.' How does that sound?"

"Good," Brose said, an edge of enthusiasm creeping into his voice. "Very good! But would any girls sign it?"

"They'll be standing in line," I told him, "if they think they may get a prom bid out of it. Do you think the fellas will come through?"

"Sure do," Brose said. "You post a petition like that on the bulletin board at school and you'll start an avalanche. We'll get publicity in the *E-Hi-News,* too. How about getting us up a slogan, something like 'Bring the prom down to earth'?"

"Wonderful!" I exclaimed. A sudden thought struck

me. "And to think, if it hadn't been for your knocking over Mr. Tareyton's nut case we might never have had this terrific brainstorm."

"Speaking of nuts," Brose said a shade sheepishly, digging a hand into his pocket, "have some?"

He brought out a little waxed paper bag filled with fresh roasted nuts and offered them to me. We both broke into hilarious laughter.

3

The petition

IF BROSE HADN'T DONE MOST OF HIS French assignment in study hall that afternoon, he never would have finished it. Because neither of us could concentrate on dull pages of translation when we were simply popping with excitement over our scheme to get the prom down to a level where more kids could afford it. Including us! We told my parents a little about what we had in mind as soon as we got back to our house. And they were enthusiastic, too.

"A very sound idea," my father beamed. "These school affairs are getting entirely out of hand. Why, it used to be a fellow could show his girl a big time if he had five dollars to spend."

"Not any more," Brose wagged his head regretfully. "But if the kids really go for this scheme of ours, it'll be a start in the right direction."

Mom's approval was based on an entirely different reason. "If you can squelch this business of chasing all the way in to Chicago after the prom," she told us, "you'll win the undying gratitude of every parent I know."

"Don't say that!" I exclaimed in mock horror. "You want to put a hex on the whole idea? Just let it get around that the parents are back of this and it'll mean the kiss of death."

I laughed then, but there was a grain of truth in my words just the same. And Mom knew it. We understand each other, Mom and I. She is a very comfortable parent to have. Dad, too, for that matter. Neither of them has forgotten, as some parents seem prone to do, that they were young once themselves.

"Pretend I didn't say it," Mom whispered, smiling.

Brose's eyes held what I took for a glint of admiration as he looked from her to my father. "And you won't mind if Tobey turns your living room into an imitation night club?" he asked.

Mom shook her head. "It's her living room, too."

My father asked, his brows rising inquiringly, "With floor show? Seems as if a night club ought to have a floor show."

A sudden idea struck me. I stared at Brose. "The Hits and Misses!" I exclaimed. "They just might be willing."

Brose chuckled. "Never knew that bunch of hams to turn down a chance to put on a show yet."

The Hits and Misses is an outgrowth of our more serious school Drama Club. Its members sing and dance and clown around generally, filling in at assemblies and whenever any other opportunity offers itself. Maybe they would put on some sort of floor show after the prom, at the various parties. It was just the sort of screwy thing that might appeal to them.

"That's a dreamy idea, Dad!" I exclaimed. "We'll certainly try to take advantage of it."

"You will?" my father asked in surprise, as though he

hadn't quite kept up with me. "I mean—what idea?"

"The floor show," I explained patiently. "But first Brose and I have to work out this petition for the girls to sign. We have to begin at the beginning. . . ."

Walking to school the next morning with my closest friend, Barbie Walters, I naturally told her all about our post-prom plans. Barbie is dark and vivacious and she completely disproves the verse about men never making passes at girls who wear glasses. She is very popular and has plenty of dates, including one for the prom with Sox Trevor. In fact, she and Sox have been saving their money toward double-dating for all the festivities with Brose and me. But she had already heard from Sox about Brose's disastrous encounter with the nut case and was prepared to let me weep on her shoulder. Only she found, to her astonishment, that I wasn't in need of comforting at all. By the time I had briefed her on Brose's and my terrific scheme and had explained about the petition we had worked out, she was as enthusiastic as I.

"It's simply quite!" Barbie exclaimed, her eyes dancing with excitement. "It's the quitest thing that's happened around school in ages! Why, Tobey, you'll be a heroine, like Joan of Arc or somebody! You know how the girls have been moaning over the boys hanging back and resisting all their wiles and hints about the prom. And they know the reason is mainly financial, but no girl can come out individually and say, 'Look now! I don't care whether you make a big production of prom night. All I want is to get to the prom itself and to heck with all the glamour stuff afterward.' I mean she'd feel too degraded. But if a lot of girls take a stand together and sign your petition, including some of us who already have dates, but who are willing to go a little easy on our guys' pocketbooks—" she broke off to stare at me inquiringly. "You are going to sign it yourself, aren't you?"

"Of course," I told her, unfolding the petition I had stuck in my Math book and showing it to her. It was worded almost exactly as Brose and I had planned from the start. And there was "Tobey Heydon" in my most flourishing scrawl on the very top line.

"Okay," Barbie said, unscrewing the cap of her pen and steadying the petition on her notebook, "this makes two of us, anyway. And will poor Sox ever be relieved! Now he can go back to eating lunches in the cafeteria again instead of bringing sandwiches from home in a paper bag."

All the rest of the way to school, we discussed ideas for turning various girls' houses into supper clubs, after the prom. "Kit Martin will have a party, I'll bet," Barbie suggested. "She's stuck without a date and they've got that big rumpus room at her house. She was telling me only yesterday that she was sure the reason Tod Jennings had let her down was because he was too flat to bear the expenses. Kit was so desperate she was thinking of offering to go Dutch, only she didn't want to hurt his pride. This is going to solve things for a lot of people. And it'll be fun, too. Gee, Tobey, how do you dream up such things?"

There was a note of genuine admiration in Barbie's voice. I told her, with becoming modesty, "Why, it's nothing, really. Any girl whose boy friend had to spend all his cash for fresh roasted nuts could think of something just as clever."

At Edgewood High you have to get permission from someone in authority before you put up a notice of any kind on the big bulletin board. Luckily, I caught up with our principal, Mr. Bleeker, in the corridor just outside his office. Mr. Bleeker has been the head of our school ever since it began in a couple of rooms upstairs over the bank and has seen it grow to its present enrollment of almost a thousand students. A job like his either seems to have the effect of mellowing a person, or turning him into a crotchety old fuss-button. Mr. Bleeker is definitely the mellowing kind, although he can be firm when necessary and doesn't let the students get away with murder. He is generally liked and respected. The fact that I didn't feel a moment's hesitation about explaining our post-prom idea to him and showing him the petition Brose and I had worked out speaks well for his sympathy and understanding.

He listened to all I had to say and read the petition through before speaking. Then he took off his shell-rimmed glasses and stood there tapping the side of his nose with them, in a way he has when he's thinking. But after a moment he grinned and scrawled "OK, Bleeker" along the edge of the petition.

"I'm glad you thought of this," he told me in his deceptively gruff voice. "I'm in favor of anything that brings these school parties back to a sensible level, where all the seniors can get in on the fun. Night clubs, all this hoop-la after the prom—well, there's no actual harm in it but it doesn't make sense. It just tends to take away the importance of the prom itself, which should be the main attraction. But coming from me, nobody'd listen to such ideas. So you work it out. More power to you."

"Thanks, Mr. Bleeker. We'll do all we can."

We stood there for a minute, grinning at each other like a pair of conspirators. Then I hurried back to where Barbie was waiting. She looked at me inquiringly and I nodded.

"Good old Bleekie," Barbie said. "I knew he'd come

through. Let's tack it up now and see the reaction."

Almost before I'd inserted the last thumbtack, there was a little clot of curious students clustered around. Barbie and I found ourselves swamped with questions, so we proceeded to talk the scheme up in a big way. But soon we realized we were wasting our breath. Further promotion wasn't necessary. Already most of the senior girls within seeing or hearing distance were hunting for pencils so they could sign their names below Barbie's and mine. This wasn't so astonishing, really, when you consider that about half of them still didn't have dates for the prom. And even some of the lucky ones knew how rough the financial going was for the boys and were willing to take it easy.

Mary Andrews, for whom I do not care ever since last year when she made a big play for Brose, but who I must admit is one of the more popular girls in our class, strolled up with her current flame, Miles Keller, in tow.

Mary glanced over the petition in that bored way of hers, which she imagines is the height of sophistication. Then, looking up at Miles for agreement, she exclaimed, "How quaint! No night club after the prom? I can't even imagine it, can you?"

Some of the girls in the crowd gave her dirty looks.

And Miles answered, with what sounded to me like a slightly wistful note in his voice. "What are they trying to do, go back to the Good Old Days, or something?"

An annoyed male voice said from the fringe of the group, "You got more money than brains, boy? Don't you know a good thing when you see it?"

A heated argument seemed on the verge of developing. But Mary managed to get Miles away before he realized he was definitely in the minority among the boys around the bulletin board.

Trust Mary, I thought, to hold out for all the trimmings. And there were bound to be others like her. Still, the scramble to sign up continued until the bell rang for classes and everyone had to hurry off. . . .

By noon the petition was full of signatures and some enterprising soul had stuck up a sheet of blank paper for the overflow. Brose's and my progress through the school cafeteria resembled a triumphal march. Barbie must have spread the word that we were the leaders of the revolt against squandering a lot of money on prom night. And apparently we had struck a very popular note. Ever so many girls confided to me that they had prom dates, as of some time this morning. And Brose's shoulder was sore from the enthusiastic whacks it received.

"Gee," he said, as we unloaded our trays at our usual table, "it looks like we really started something."

I nodded. "I guess practically the whole senior class was ripe for revolution."

"Only no one would probably have done anything about it," Brose beamed at me, "if it weren't for you. I can't take much credit. I really kind of backed into the whole thing."

"It was Mr. Tareyton's nut counter you backed into," I laughed. "But that was our inspiration. If the scheme goes over, we'll both take the credit. But if it flops, we'll share the blame."

"All for one and one for all," Brose said staunchly.

"Okay, you three musketeers minus one," Barbie's voice drawled behind me, "slide over and give us room."

"Yeah," Sox Trevor said, "let us bask in your reflected glory. We knew you before you were such big shots, remember?"

Brose asked, "You want my autograph, boy?"

"Shush, you two," Barbie interrupted their clowning. "Tobey and I have stuff to discuss." Her eyes were shining with excitement as she asked, "Do you realize what you've started?"

I admitted, "Well, I hear a lot of dates were made for the prom this morning."

Barbie nodded. "It's snowballing. Why, even girls who were all set to do the town are climbing on the band wagon. After all, they don't want their dates to consider them mercenary. Of course, there are some hold-outs, but who cares?" She rushed on, "Half a dozen girls are already planning parties. We ought to get up a committee to figure out details, decide which night clubs to call the various houses and what kind of show we want the Hits and Misses to put on and—"

"A committee," Sox broke in, "is a group of the unfit, appointed by the unwilling, to take care of the unnecessary. Just a little gem of wisdom I picked up on the radio."

Brose laughed and even Barbie and I weakened and smiled. But we had more important things than radio humor to devote our attention to. If that wasn't just like a man, I thought. Neither Sox nor Brose had the vaguest idea of all the work our post-prom plans involved. But they'd find out. We'd all have to keep humping to get the whole project into shape. And we only had a couple of weeks to do it in, too.

It was a shame Brose couldn't have had his accident a little sooner.

4

Preliminaries

ITCHY STEARNS IS THE EDITOR OF OUR weekly school paper and it was he who dreamed up the catchy name, Operation Night Club. The *E-Hi-News* came out two days after we had posted our petition and the project rated a front page spread, no less. SENIOR GIRLS GET SMART, read the headline. And, beneath that in only slightly smaller print, "Home Parties After Prom Ease Finances, Increase Dates." There was an editorial that waxed positively lyrical in its approval of our scheme. Opinions from prominent seniors were quoted and, while a few hold-outs insisted that the prom would lose half its glamour without a supper club finale, they were overwhelmingly outnumbered. The paper went on to say that a dozen or more post-prom parties were being planned, with a night club motif in each case. Moreover, these parties would be enlivened by floor shows in which members of the Hits and Misses would take part. All in all, it sounded as though Operation Night Club had caught on.

It made all of us involved in the proceedings feel pretty

good. But if time had seemed to pass quickly before, it was really jet-propelled now. Luckily Barbie is the executive type and thrives on problems. And Brose and Sox did the best they could to help, in their slightly bumbling male way. Between the four of us and a growing gang of enthusiastic supporters, we gradually got things pretty well whipped into shape.

It wouldn't have been so rugged if we hadn't had our schoolwork to keep up, too. But with finals looming ahead, we couldn't afford to relax on that score. Teachers are so unco-operative about things like finals. So between all the prom activities and Brose's French and my math, things really got a little hectic. There were moments when I felt beat right down to my saddle shoes and I knew all the others felt the same way.

"At least," Barbie reminded me in one of our snatched moments of relaxation over chocolate malteds, "you don't have a dress to buy besides everything else. I have tried on formals till I'm out of my mind and I still can't find one that does a thing for me!"

I thought with pleasure of my delectable aqua dress, strapless and with yards and yards of skirt, which I had kept zipped up carefully in a garment bag since the college dance to which I had worn it last fall. It was fabulously becoming and Dick Allen, who had invited me up to Central for a football week end had been properly impressed with it. Brose hadn't even seen it yet, nor had any of my friends except Barbie. I was looking forward to wearing it to the prom with as much happy anticipation as though it had been brand new.

I told Barbie, "You're too fussy, that's your trouble."

But Barbie shook her head. "No, I'm not. It's just that a girl has to look her best for the senior prom if she's ever going to. There's a blue paper taffeta at Wentworth's I like quite well. But you know what a hag I look in blue."

"Couldn't they order one for you in a different color?"

"They offered to get it in yellow," Barbie admitted. "But then I'd be afraid someone else might buy the blue and two of us would turn up at the prom dressed alike except for the color."

Her tone indicated that this would be a fate worse than death and, knowing that I'd have felt that way, too, under the same circumstances, I nodded in agreement. But I didn't pay too much attention as Barbie continued to discuss the pros and cons of prom dresses. Actually my thoughts were busy with plans for ways to turn our living room into a reasonable facsimile of the Chez Paree. Kit Martin was going to have the Empire Room and various other Chicago night spots were going to be unveiled in Edgewood on prom night, although their proprietors weren't remotely aware of it. Each hostess would serve supper at card tables, arranged around a cleared space of floor for dancing. Rugs would be rolled back, furniture rearranged, lights dimmed provocatively. All the parents involved were proving quite co-operative. I guess, like Mom and Dad, they considered the inconvenience of having their houses torn apart for an evening a small price to pay for the peace of mind of knowing that their off-spring wouldn't be driving all the way in to the city after the dance.

During the days that followed, Barbie finally found the dress of her dreams at a shop in Chicago. And gradually most of the other worrisome details of the big evening ironed themselves out. All of us concerned got a large charge out of the ticket committee's announcement on the Friday before the prom that the dance would be better attended than any senior prom in years. It seemed all the seniors capable of distinguishing a waltz from a rhumba would be there.

Mr. Bleeker caught up with Brose and me in the corridor after the assembly at which the announcement had been made. He laid a big hand on my shoulder and one on Brose's and murmured, "Good work!" before hurrying on his way.

"Now what was that for?" Brose asked, when Mr. Bleeker was out of hearing distance.

"He approves of Operation Night Club," I confided to Brose. "I told you that before."

"Well, we just better keep it under our hats," Brose said warningly, as if I didn't know. . . .

Saturday morning Barbie and Sox and Brose and I worked like dogs rearranging our living room into a night club. Mom left this entirely up to me, preferring to devote her whole attention to the refreshments. Midge got underfoot a good deal, in that indescribably helpful way little sisters have. But with Barbie and Brose and Sox all in there pitching, we managed to accomplish a good deal in spite of her.

The effect we finally achieved was quite striking, although whether it actually resembled the Chez Paree or not, we weren't sure, since none of us had been there. But it was all very French, with chalk murals thumb-tacked to the walls and a chummy little space for dancing in the middle of all our borrowed card tables and chairs.

My mother sort of gasped when she came in and saw it for the first time. But she is a good scout and recovered quickly.

"Very—nice," she said brightly. "You'd hardly recognize it for a living room, would you?"

"That's the idea," I explained patiently. "If it looked like a living room, we'd have failed."

My mother nodded, a faint frown between her eyes. "And hardly anyone is likely to drop in on a Saturday afternoon."

"Of course not," I assured her.

We all trooped out to the kitchen then, because it was almost noon and we were practically starving from all the work we'd done. We made Dagwoods out of stuff we found in the refrigerator, ham and cheese and pickles and sandwich spread and such. And Mom gave us milk and fresh-baked cookies. The four of us got quite silly and hilarious, with Midge and Mom joining in the fun. My father was out of town on a business trip, or he'd have been right in the thick of it, as there is nothing Dad likes better than a crowd of people being informal around the kitchen table.

Afterward we cleaned up the mess we'd made, declining Mom's help. Barbie and I washed and dried the dishes, while Brose and Sox went through the motions of giving us assistance. Actually all they did was to get in our way. Sometimes I wonder if men are really as awkward around a kitchen as they seem, or whether it is just a fiendishly clever act they put on so as not to be expected to do much work.

Later, we sat for a while on the porch, lazy and relaxed in the afternoon sunshine. We started talking about school and how soon our last year at Edgewood High would be over.

"Just think," Brose said, "in less than a month, we'll be alumni."

"We hope!" Sox said with feeling.

"They'd have let us know by now," Barbie reassured

him, "if we weren't going to make it. Any of us."

"I don't know," Sox said darkly. "Sometimes Miss Leveritt gets a kind of mean gleam in her eye when I flub an answer. It makes me wonder if she's getting ready to let the axe fall."

But Barbie shook her head positively in the negative. "You'd have got a pink slip with your last report card if you were on thin ice."

"I'll bet we're all as good as graduated right now," I backed her up.

Brose chose to look on the dark side, along with Sox. "I'm not taking a thing for granted," he said, "till I get that nice white diploma clutched in my hot little hand."

"Can't you just see us all," I murmured dreamily, "walking up the aisle in our caps and gowns?"

Somehow the thought made me feel a little sad, a bit lost, although there was no denying that graduation was the main aim and purpose of our years at high school. Looking back, it didn't seem so long ago that we had all been freshmen, childish and awkward and unsure of ourselves. Barbie and I had been good friends even then, but we had scarcely known Brose and Sox. Looking at Brose, slumped beside me on the glider, his dark head resting on the back-cushion, his long legs stuck out before him, I felt very close to him, very warm and happy to know he liked me, that we were such good friends. But with graduation, lots of things would be changed. We'd have passed a milestone along the road to growing up. Then there'd be college, jobs, a whole new way of living. Who could tell what the future held for Brose and me, for any of us?

"Now wait!" Barbie said drily. "Don't get us into caps and gowns yet. I'd rather picture me in my new formal tonight."

"Dripping with orchids," Sox put in, expanding his chest proudly. "I could afford two of 'em on account of not having to save enough money to go night-clubbing."

"Tobey's only going to drip with carnations," Brose said a shade wistfully. "On account of everybody knows what."

I patted his hand. "I love carnations," I assured him. "Orchids wouldn't go with my dress, anyway."

"They will with mine," Barbie smiled. "I planned it that way."

Sox, who had apparently been following up a train of thought brought on by Brose's remark, inquired hopefully, "Did you eat all those nuts, Brose? I could go for some of 'em right now."

Brose shook his head. "They're all gone. And frankly, I'm glad. They reminded me of a dark chapter in my life, which I prefer to forget."

We lolled there, laughing and gabbing, unaware of the passage of time until Barbie happened to glance at her wrist watch.

"Jeepers!" she exclaimed, getting hastily to her feet. "It's three o'clock!"

"So what?" Sox asked, lifting one eyebrow.

"I have to go home," Barbie informed him, "and start getting ready."

"For tonight?" Sox stared up at her incredulously.

"You don't fondly imagine," Barbie inquired, "that a girl gets all glamoured up for a prom in a half hour or so, do you?"

Sox admitted, "I always kind of figured you just started to dress when I rang the doorbell, you keep me waiting so long."

"Very funny!" Barbie glared at him.

Sox took warning from her tone and didn't kid her any more. I was glad. It would be a shame if they got into an argument a few hours before the prom, but such things have been known to happen.

As Sox stood up to leave with Barbie, Brose asked me, "Do I have to scram, too?"

"I guess you'd better," I smiled at him. "I've got just as much to do as Barbie has."

Brose and Sox exchanged one of those long rueful looks of understanding that men love to annoy girls with.

"Women!" Brose sighed, shaking his head.

"You said it," Sox agreed.

"You want us different?" Barbie asked.

And I added, "Any little improvements you'd care to suggest?"

"Nah," Brose said, his warm grin and the gleam in his dark eyes making my heart beat quite a bit faster. "We're used to you this way."

It wasn't what he said, but the way he said it. He can be very sweet. . . .

5

Prom night

THE SENIOR PROM IS SOMETHING A GIRL doesn't ever want to forget, never as long as she lives. At least, that was the way I felt about it. From the very beginning it was one of those star-dusted occasions, one of those nights you wish you could put away intact in a special compartment of your mind and take out every now and then to dream over.

Midge sort of infiltrated into my room while I was dressing. She was wearing jeans and a grubby tee-shirt and she sprawled across the foot of the bed, intent on my every move. She seemed unusually quiet and there was such a wistful expression on her freckled little face, I suspected she must be looking forward to the time when she'd be getting ready for a prom herself. The thought gave me a queer feeling. Why, Midge was just a baby, although she'd have socked me if I'd dared to say such a thing out loud. But she wasn't eleven yet. Still, I could remember how it had been when I was little, how I'd watched my older sisters get ready for dances and had dreamed and wondered about it all deep down inside me. Now here I was and here was Midge, with the process repeating itself, as if a wheel was turning. And Janet and Alicia were both married and away from home. Janet even had two children.

The realization of how quickly time passed and things changed made my throat ache for a minute. But then I remembered the awful congestion in the bathrooms when four of us girls were around, and what stinkers Alicia and Janet used to be if I borrowed their clothes or lipsticks. That made the queer sad lump in my throat go away and I felt happy again.

I reached out the stopper of my perfume bottle and put a dab of scent on Midge's hand. She sniffed it appreciatively.

"Yum," she said. "Is it the stuff Brose gave you Valentine's Day?"

I nodded. "But don't imagine you can get away with helping yourself, just because I'm so generous tonight."

"I won't," my little sister said with unnatural meekness. Then a kind of dreamy, questioning look crossed her face and she said, "Tobey?"

"Yes?" I went on brushing my hair, but our eyes met in the dressing table mirror.

"Tobey, is it awful terrific to go to a prom? Or do you get sort of used to it—I mean, when you've been to lots of dances like you have?"

"It's still terrific," I told her, smiling a little. "I love dances. And, of course, the senior prom's such a *very* special occasion—well, it overshadows all the rest."

"Even that college dance you went to with Dick?" Midge pressed eagerly.

She takes a special interest in my occasional dates with Dick Allen. This is easy to understand, since his little sister, Judy, is Midge's closest friend. In fact, it was through those two and a kind of comedy of errors arising out of the Heart Hop last year that Dick and I met.

"That was pretty special, too," I admitted. "But—oh, I don't know. There's just something about the senior prom. All the time you're in high school you see it looming away up there ahead of you. And you wonder when you're a freshman if you'll get asked to it at all. And then, when you get a little more self-confidence and have a few dates, you wonder who'll take you and what you'll wear and everything. You'll find out how it is."

Midge sighed so deeply that her chest pushed her messy tee-shirt out in a kind of swell. "Yeah," she murmured dreamily. "Yeah, I guess so. . . ."

Mom came in to help me get into my dress and zip it up for me. And her eyes were sort of shining, too, just as Midge's and mine were. I guess a senior prom is pretty wonderful from any angle, whether you're going to it, or looking back on it, or looking forward to it. There seemed to be a kind of warmth, a togetherness, wrapping Mom and Midge and me about, making me feel good inside.

"You look sweet," Mom said. "I think that's the prettiest formal you've ever had, dear." A slightly worried frown pulled her brows together for just a minute. "You're quite sure those little stays in the bodice top—"

"Now, Mom," I gave her a quick hug, "don't worry. I've worn this during one whole dance, remember? There's not the slightest danger."

Midge said admiringly, "I don't see how you keep it up, without even a teensy strap." She glanced down at her own flat little front disgustedly and Mom and I restrained an impulse to laugh.

"You'll find out," I told her, giving her shoulder an

affectionate pat. "Now I've got to get downstairs."

"Oh, my goodness!" Mom exclaimed, appalled. "That was what I came up to tell you, that Brose was here."

I'd heard him come in myself, a good fifteen minutes earlier. But tonight he didn't seem to mind that I'd kept him waiting. He had been sitting at one of the card tables in our transformed living room and, as he heard Mom and Midge and me approaching along the hall, he exclaimed loudly, "The service in this restaurant sure is lousy—" then, as he caught a glimpse of me, he broke off to say, "Wow!" with flattering emphasis.

"You like it?" I asked, turning around for inspection like a fashion model.

"And how!" Brose grinned, getting to his feet.

He looked very handsome in his new birthday dinner jacket, that wasn't too short in the sleeves as his old one had been. He handed me a lovely yellow carnation corsage in a cellophane box and I thanked him and exclaimed over it.

"See how it goes with my dress?" I held it up against me. "But I'll carry it till we get there, so my coat won't crush it."

I gave Mom a few last minute instructions and told her about what time to expect us back, along with the other seven couples who would make up my party for supper.

"Can I stay up and see?" Midge was dancing up and down in her excitement.

Mom smiled, patting her shoulder. "It'll be much too late, honey. But you got to see Tobey and Brose."

"And we're the best looking." Brose winked at her.

We said good night then and left. For once the weather was on our side instead of trying to spoil everything. The night was crisply cool, starlit. The moon rode round and pale above the dark of the treetops. The air held the fresh sweet scent of growing things.

"Hi," Brose said softly, as we settled ourselves in his family's car, parked on the drive.

"Hi," I murmured back.

"You look terrific," he told me.

"So do you," I said and lifted my lips as he leaned nearer.

As always, his kiss had quite an unsettling effect on me. You'd think I might be used to it by this time, but I'm not. I guess I never will be.

After a minute I leaned back, with a happy, rather breathless little sigh. "Well," I said, "this is it."

"Yeah," Brose nodded, turning on the ignition. "The big night."

I felt as you do in a theater, when the orchestra begins tuning up for the overture. Expectant, hushed, all warm and bubbly with anticipation. As we backed out into the street and Brose swung the car around to head for Barbie's house, where we were picking up Sox and her, I thought I had never felt more perfectly happy in my life. But then a small doubt flashed on like a warning light in my mind. What if Operation Night Club proved a colossal flop? What if all the kids who were giving parties and the ones who were going to them were doomed to be disappointed and to wish they'd gone night-clubbing after all? We'd be to blame, Brose and I, because we'd dreamed up the idea. Butterflies began playing tag in my tummy.

But before I could open my mouth to speak, Brose said, as though he'd seen right into my mind, "Relax, baby. It'll be okay, you'll see. Everything is going to work out just fine."

He sounded exactly as my father does when he's trying

to soothe Mom out of one of the tizzies she occasionally gets into. And, just as Mom does, I found his unreasonable male confidence maddeningly annoying.

"How can you be so sure?" I demanded, glaring at him.

"Got a hunch," Brose confided and grinned.

His grin isn't easy to resist. I felt my fears fading.

And he proved right.

The prom was wonderful! The decorations committee had done a really terrific job on the country club ballroom, working out a carousel theme. Big silver cut-outs of horses, with sweeping white manes and tails, were spaced around the walls. There were gaily colored reproductions of old-fashioned caliopes and great clusters of bright balloons. The music proved to be worth all we'd paid for it and it set the tempo for a very gala mood. But the thing that made Brose and me feel especially good, as if we'd accomplished something worth while, was that practically all the seniors were on hand. Boys who had to work hard at after-school jobs, some I couldn't remember ever having seen at a dance before, were there with their dates, having a grand time.

"You see?" Brose murmured in my ear. "Didn't I tell you?"

"You and your hunches," I said around the silly lump in my throat. But my smile was so warm he blinked a little.

Afterward, at our house, everything went off wonderfully well. Mom had really outdone herself on the refreshments and Barbie's mother had come over to help. We got lots of compliments on our mad French murals. Everyone entered into the spirit of the occasion and when the Hits and Misses floor show turned up, we all gave it a rousing welcome. The troupe put on a good show, too, and it only added to the fun when one of the dancers tripped over someone's foot—after all, the space was a bit crowded—and landed squarely in Sox's lap!

It was Barbie who had the absolutely dazzling idea of "doing the town" and going on to the other houses where night-club parties were being held, in order to mix the crowds up and keep things at a high pitch. A few phone calls to the other hostesses started the ball rolling. Then we all piled into cars and split up, some to go to Kit Martin's Empire Room, some to Jane Morrell's Pump Room and so on, while kids from those parties headed for our house or one of the others.

By the time all the festivities were over, it was as late as it would have been if we'd all gone in to Chicago. And this was a good thing, because you just can't go home early on prom night. Everyone knows that. But we all agreed we couldn't have had more fun. And the cost had been so small, it hadn't put a serious dent in any boy's finances. We felt we might have established a precedent for other years, for other senior classes that would follow after us.

Brose and I lingered on our porch for a few minutes, saying good night and discussing the wonderful evening. My feet ached so from dancing, I was carrying my slippers in one hand. I liked the feel of Brose's arms around me, but I was so tired my eyelids felt sandpapery and I let my head droop wearily against his shoulder.

"Tonight," Brose said solemnly, "we have made a tradition at Edgewood High."

"Ummm," I agreed, yawning.

It sounded very impressive and I shouldn't be surprised if it were true, but at the moment I was just too sleepy to care. . . .

6

Graduation blues

SCHOOL BUZZED WITH REMINISCENT EXcitement over the prom for a few days. Then things settled down to normal, if you could call final exams normal. But before long those were over, too, which only goes to prove that no matter how horrible anything is, it can't last forever. I didn't do nearly so badly as I had feared I might in math. Nor did Brose quite flunk French, for which I felt I deserved some sort of minor medal.

Apparently Brose thought so, too. When he showed me the C he had squeaked through with on his report card, he said wryly, "I guess that belongs to you more than it does to me."

One thing you can say for Brose, he is always appreciative.

"Oh, well," I smiled at him, "look how you saved my neck in math."

Brose grinned, too. "Why does a girl need to know math, anyway? So long as you can balance our checkbook."

That "our" threw my heart for a loss, so that it had to

beat faster for a minute to catch up. When Brose talks that way, as if we're going to get married later on, it makes me feel sort of soft and quivery inside. But I hoped it didn't show.

"What do you think I'll be marrying *you* for—if I do," I inquired, "except to balance our checkbook."

"Fine thing!" Brose said. But his hand closed around mine as we walked along.

The spring days were warm and sweet and they seemed to melt away as quickly as ice cubes in a defrosting refrigerator. And suddenly all our crowd was caught up in the hectic excitement and activity of Graduation Week. So many things happened so quickly, too quickly, some gay and silly, some solemn and thought provoking, all to be filed away and never quite forgotten, even if I lived to be an old, old woman.

Scribbling like mad in everyone's yearbook, getting yours scribbled in, in return. The baccalaureate sermon, with the minister's white head shining in a single shaft of sunlight that seemed to seek him out like a finger, while his rich warm voice flowed out over us all. Take-over Day, which is a school tradition, with the seniors sitting in for teachers and principal. The regular faculty goes around to classes with the rest of the students, heckling us and getting even for the rough time we've given them. During one memorable period on Take-over Day I taught, to use the word loosely, math, of all subjects. How I lived through it, I'll never know. And Brose had the honor of assuming Mr. Bleeker's exalted duties for an hour. The day was a riot for all concerned and led, as it always does, to a fine glow of good feeling between students and teachers.

One of the highlights of Graduation Week was the class picnic. We got the day off from school for this and it was super-terrific. Everyone turned up in jeans and loaded down with lunch baskets, thermos bottles, blankets, record-players and ukuleles. The weather forecast was "Cloudy, with showers" and the weather bureau wasn't fooling. But we didn't let it dampen our enthusiasm, although there were a couple of times during the morning we had to interrupt our games and hold the blankets over our heads like tents, or get under trees or into cars for shelter. But by early afternoon, the skies had begun to clear. We gathered enough dry wood to build a lovely big fire and sprawled around it, eating ourselves into a pleasant lethargy, singing songs and yacking.

Everyone was gay, but there was a sort of nostalgic thread running through our gayety. A feeling of finality, an awareness of changes lying ahead, hung over us. Lots of the talk was of college, of enlistments, of jobs. Some of the couples we knew were engaged; they were planning to marry before too long.

"Nothing will be quite the same after this week," Sox Trevor said. "We won't be seniors any more, we won't be bound together by the mere fact of being in the same class at school."

Barbie said, "It gives you a kind of queer feeling, doesn't it? Kind of—sad."

I nodded. "It's silly, of course. But somehow I just feel as if I love everyone in the class, even the ones I've never liked very well. I hate to think of us all breaking up, going off in different directions."

"If you want to cry on my shoulder," Brose teased, touching his jacket, "here's a good soft spot." But I could tell by the look in his eyes that he knew exactly what I meant and that he felt the same way. Only boys always think they have to be so strong and untouched by emotion that he wouldn't come right out and admit it.

Someone started singing the Whiffenpoof Song then. And there is something about that tune that always gets me, anyway. As everyone joined in and the haunting melody poured out, there in the green quiet of the woods, it seemed to me that I was going to burst right out crying. But if I'd done a thing like that, I'd never have been able to live it down, so I managed to blink back the tears.

Brose's fingers closing tight around mine and the sort of gentle way he looked at me, not laughing or anything, helped. . . .

Almost before it seemed possible, our last days at Edgewood High were over and it was Graduation Night. My sister Alicia and her husband, Adam Wentworth, drove down for the occasion from Central University, where Adam is studying medicine. The thought of their doing that, just to see me graduated, gave me a nice warm glow. Alicia and I didn't get along so well before she was married. She is quite beautiful in an ash-blond, languid sort of way and our personalities are sort of antagonistic, I guess, although she has mellowed a lot under Adam's influence and I don't think she's nearly as difficult as she used to be. Maybe I've grown up some, too. We haven't had a scrap in ages, but that could be due to the fact that we don't see so much of each other any more.

"Just think," Alicia said at dinner that night, "of Tobey being through school. It just doesn't seem possible!"

"Oh, I don't know," Adam grinned at me. "I thought she'd make it eventually."

"That wasn't what I meant," Alicia said. She hasn't much of a sense of humor. She went on, "Why, it doesn't seem any time ago that Janet and I were having a horrible time, trying to keep her from using our lipsticks and wearing our best Nylons and—"

"Okay, okay," I said. "So I was a brat. But you have to admit you and Janet were a little stinky, too, the way you treated me, as if I were an idiot child, or something."

"Like you treat me?" Midge asked wickedly.

After our laughter had subsided, Dad said, "You see, girls, it's a vicious circle. First Janet had Alicia in her hair, then Alicia and Janet had Tobey. And now Tobey has Midge. The wear and tear on your mother and me has been terrific."

"Oh, I don't know," Mom chuckled. "I get a kind of kick out of seeing the way situations repeat themselves. I've developed a philosophical attitude toward the whole business."

"Is that what it is?" I teased her. "I thought you were just getting calloused."

It was fun, having so many of the family together around the dinner table. I found myself wishing that Janet and her husband, Jim, and their two children didn't live so far away. I hadn't seen little Jimmy since they'd moved to California. And I'd never seen the baby at all, and she was almost six months old now.

We lingered longer over dessert than we should have. I had quite a rush, getting into my white dress, doing all the last minute details I'd left till after dinner. Alicia came up to help me and so did Mom and Midge, so the congestion in my room got pretty thick and I began to wonder if I wouldn't have got along faster by myself. But they were all enjoying themselves so much, I didn't have the heart to say so.

Eventually, we all got to school and I left my family

while I hurried off to the room in which the senior girls were to put on their caps and gowns. It was a mad melee of chatter and laughter and half-hysterical shrieking. How we ever got organized, I'll never know, but eventually we were lined up, ready but jittery, outside the auditorium doors.

The big room was filled to the bursting point with proud, but perspiring parents and friends. There seems to be a universal law that graduation night must always be unseasonably hot. We just about expired in those long gowns and the mortar-board caps felt as if they were welded to our brows as we walked down the endless aisle to the slow strains of "Edgewood Forever." Surely the auditorium hadn't ever been so big before?

I caught a glimpse of Mom and Dad and Midge and Alicia and Adam, all craning their necks interestedly in my direction. All I could manage was a rather tremulous smile as I passed by.

Once settled in our tiered seats on the platform, we all felt we could relax a little, but not much. Although the audience was just a mass of unidentifiable faces beyond the footlights, we felt as self-conscious as goldfish in a bowl. But gradually, as everything went along just as it had at rehearsal, we began to feel a bit easier, to look around unobtrusively and take notice of where our particular friends were sitting. Brose was in the row immediately behind me and he kept giving me little shoves and nudges and whispering ridiculous things into my ear which made it hard for me to act dignified.

Then the main speaker began to talk. He was a senator who had gone to Edgewood High himself ages ago. He proved to be more interesting than we had dared to hope and a lot of the things he said made good sense, instead of being just a lot of lofty generalities as so many graduation speeches are. Or maybe his remarks seemed to have a special impact because we were the ones he was talking about, the ones on the verge of going out from the familiar shelter of school into the big unknown world. Anyway, he didn't talk too long and for that we were grateful.

I was sure my nose must be shiny from the heat by the time my name was called and I got up and walked across the platform to receive my diploma and Mr. Bleeker's smiling handshake. But it was no shinier than anyone else's nose, so I didn't care.

Afterwards, everyone got very talkative and hilarious in the thronged corridor outside the auditorium. Families knotted into little clumps around their own particular graduate, laughing and congratulatory. Kids waved their diplomas gleefully in the air and there were lots of exclamations echoing around, such as "Yippee, I made it!" and "Never thought I'd live to see the day!"

But beneath all the din and exuberance, you could sense a layer of solemnity that no one quite wanted to admit or acknowledge. After all, this was an important occasion in our lives, an end and a beginning, just as the senator had said. But it would have been too corny to come right out and say so among ourselves. Still, the realization was there, deep down inside us all, and inside our parents, too. Mom sounded sort of chokey, I thought, as she asked Brose and his parents to stop by at our house for some coffee and cake and ice cream. And Mrs. Gilman's voice didn't sound entirely natural as she accepted Mom's invitation.

Dad patted Brose's father on the back and said, almost too heartily, "Well, I guess we'll have to take a back seat from here on in and let these new graduates see what they can do with the world."

"I guess so," Mr. Gilman said in his precise way.

He glanced at Brose and there seemed to be a sort of surprised look on his face, as though Brose had sneaked behind his back in some way and grown up before he'd quite had time to get used to the idea.

"It just doesn't seem possible," Mrs. Gilman said, so it seemed her thoughts must have been following the same vein. "Why, it can't have been four years ago they were just starting high school."

"Oh, yes, it could," Brose said firmly. "I've got the diploma to prove it, too."

"For that matter," Dad said, "it doesn't seem too long ago that *we* were in the graduating class, does it?"

As our families drifted off on a stream of reminiscence, we all moved on down the familiar corridor toward the big front door. All of them were laughing and chattering but Brose and me. We passed the Library and Mr. Bleeker's office, the Science Room, the Math Room. A queer tightness caught at my throat. I thought: Why, this is probably the last time I'll walk along this corridor, past these doors I've gone in and out of so often. It was as Brose's mother had said, it just didn't seem possible that four whole years had passed since we started high school. And despite all the griping I'd done over studying and homework and being shut up in stuffy old classrooms, it had been a rather wonderful four years and too soon over.

I swallowed hard and then I felt Brose's big hand close around mine. I looked up and his face was grave, his glance understanding. I knew then that he was feeling the same queer lost sensation that gripped me. Were all the seniors feeling it, I wondered, down underneath their too insistent laughter and gayety?

As we passed slowly through the doorway that led out

into the summer night, I reached over and gave the frame of it a surreptitious little pat. And Brose saw me do it, but he didn't even smile.

7

I reach a decision

When I woke up the next morning, all my sentimental silliness over being through high school seemed like a crazy dream.

"I must have been loopy," I said aloud as I sat up in bed, stretching and luxuriating in the warm summer breeze that billowed my ruffled curtains. "I must have been out of my mind."

Vacation was always wonderful and three whole months of it lay ahead of me. If I liked, I could lie down again and sleep for hours. Mom wouldn't wake me, I knew, this very first morning. But I felt so rested and refreshed, I had an idea it must be pretty late now. I glanced toward the mad jumble of stuff on my dresser, diploma, yearbook, some clothes, besides all the other things that actually belonged there. My alarm clock was hidden somewhere in the midst of the conglomeration. I could hear it ticking away merrily, but I couldn't see it at all.

Who cared about time anyway, I asked myself? I was free. I could be lazy, do exactly as I pleased. No more tense moments over finals, no more studying, no more rushing through breakfast to get to school on time. All the wild hassle of the last few weeks was over.

There was a silly rhyme we used to chant when we were little. Something like, "No more pencils, no more books, no more teachers' crabby looks." I laughed at the memory, then ran my spread fingers through my hair and stretched again like a lazy cat. I slid out of bed and the rug felt soft and pleasantly tickly against the soles of my feet. I could hear childish voices in the yard below, so I padded over to the window and looked out.

Midge and Judy Allen were playing a rather lackadaisical game of hopscotch on our front walk, their bare feet making little plopping noises as they landed in the chalked squares on the cement. I could remember how rough and warm the pavement used to feel under my own bare feet when I was little and what a bang I got out of shedding my shoes and socks for the first time in the spring.

A pleasant sense of kinship with the two below made me hail them cheerfully, "Hi, kids. Having fun?"

They both looked up, startled, Judy's black hair framing her rather thin face, Midge's sandy pigtails swinging.

"Oh, hi," Judy said, grinning. Her smile reminded me just a little of her brother's.

"I see you finally made it," Midge said. "I thought you were going to sleep all day."

"What time is it?" I asked.

"Late," Midge said succinctly.

And Judy elaborated, "It must be almost noon. I'm gettin' awful hungry."

That really didn't prove a thing, I thought. Judy and Midge had appetites that there seemed small hope of appeasing, no matter how much or how often they ate. Thinking of appetites, I suddenly realized I was practically starved myself.

I started to leave the window, but Midge yelled peremptorily, "Tobey, wait! We got news for you."

"Uh-huh!" Judy backed her up positively. "Big news!"

"What about?" I leaned on the sill again, curious.

"About Dick," Midge held out infuriatingly.

But Judy, too full of exciting information to dally, skipped back and forth in a kind of jittery little jig step. "You know what? He's enlisted!"

"He has?" I gasped. "But—isn't he still at college?"

Judy nodded. "Yeah, but he called up last night and told Mom and Dad all about it. He's going to enlist today in the navy. He said not knowing when he'd be drafted and all was getting him down, so he figured he might's well get into the branch he liked best."

I could understand that. Ever so many fellows I knew felt the same way. Hardly any of them expected to get more than a year or so of college before they'd be called into service.

"What did your folks say?" I asked.

Judy shrugged. "They weren't very s'prised. His letters have been full of it ever since Christmas vacation. Mom cried some after they finished talking to him. But Daddy said he'd be glad to have it settled, so Mom wouldn't be all stirred up all the time." She went on informatively, "He'll only have a couple of weeks at home, I guess, and then he'll be going to Great Lakes for his boot training."

"If he passes his physical," Midge put in.

Judy looked affronted. "He's awful healthy," she said. "Why wouldn't he pass?"

I said, "Gee, I can hardly believe it."

"That he'll pass?" Judy demanded indignantly.

"No, no," I said. "That he's going to be in the navy."

Mollified, Judy confided, "I'll bet he'll look kind of cute

in that uniform."

The same idea had just occurred to me.

Now that their news was imparted, Midge seemed to have lost interest in the conversation. She tugged at the tail of Judy's tee-shirt, which, as usual, was flying at half-mast over her shorts.

"C'mon," Midge said. "It's your turn."

They went casually back to their hopping.

I got dressed, putting on a sleeveless shirt and shorts, as I wanted to start getting a tan as soon as possible. In the kitchen, I grabbed a hasty glass of orange juice and a handful of cookies. Luckily Mom was sewing in the library, so she wasn't aware of my sketchy breakfast. But I simply had to get over to Barbie's in a hurry and tell her about Dick. News like this wouldn't keep.

Just as I reached the foot of our front steps, I saw Brose coming up the walk toward me. He had a tennis racquet under one arm and a big grin brightened his face at sight of me. Ordinarily I'm glad to see him, too. But this morning I felt a small sinking sensation at the interruption.

"Well, what do you know?" he said. "Mental telepathy. Here you are, all dressed for tennis and I hadn't even asked you yet."

"What I'm really dressed for," I told him, "is sun tanning. I was just on my way over to Barbie's."

"Oh, well," Brose said airily, "the sun's just as bright on the tennis courts as in Barbie's yard."

I couldn't deny that. So I went into the house for my racquet and we headed for the park courts. On our way, I told Brose about Dick. After all, I'd burst if I didn't tell someone and while Brose wasn't the ideal audience, he'd have to do for the time being.

"Well, blow me down," Brose said. "This'll sink the fleet for sure."

I might have known his reaction would be something like that. Brose is no more able to be objective about Dick Allen, than I can about Mary Andrews. It's something fundamental, I guess. Dick just rubs Brose the wrong way, no matter how agreeable he tries to be.

I said coolly, "That's a very infantile way to talk."

"Why?" Brose demanded. "Do I have to stand up and cheer?"

"You needn't be nasty."

Brose thought about it for a minute. Then he grinned, a slightly sheepish grin. "No, I guess I don't. But seeing you all starry-eyed over the guy—well, I resent it."

I slipped my hand into his. "I get starry-eyed over you quite often, too," I reminded.

"Not often enough," Brose griped, but his fingers tightened around mine. "I guess it's because you see so much of me."

"Oh, I don't know," I said. "I'd miss you if I didn't."

At the park, we played a couple of fast sets, both of which Brose won, in spite of my very best efforts. Naturally he was in a fine mood after that. We sprawled in the shade, resting and cooling off for a while. Brose picked a long blade of grass and tickled my knee with it.

"I've got news for you, too," he said, "but it's nothing spectacular like Dick joining the navy."

"What?" I asked, ignoring the latter part of his remark.

"I'm going to get a job," Brose informed me. "A summer job, that is. It's practically all set. I was in to see Mr. Perkins first thing this morning."

"Who's Mr. Perkins?" I asked.

"Landscape gardener," Brose explained, "tree surgeon, stuff like that."

"Calling Dr. Gilman," I laughed. "Our tree needs an operation right away."

"Scalpel," Brose laughed, too. "Anaesthesia." He sobered then. "Anyway, it's a job. And it's an outside one like I wanted. Better than office work, or hustling cases of canned goods at the grocery."

I nodded. "You'll get an elegant tan."

"Sure," Brose said, "and build up my muscles."

"I didn't know you were planning to work this summer," I told him. There was always some talk of summer jobs among our crowd, but Brose hadn't said anything very definite on the subject.

"I figured I should," Brose said. "My folks are going to have to lay out a lot of moola for college this fall. So it seemed the least I could do was to help out."

I knew what he meant. College was expensive. Even only planning to go as far away as Central, I'd had some qualms about all the money it would cost. Besides, a girl needed so many clothes.

I said, my tone thoughtful, "I wonder what my family would think of the idea of my working this summer?"

Brose looked up at me in surprise. "You mean it?"

"I don't see why not." The idea appealed to me more by the minute. "Maybe Barbie'd like to get a job, too. Then we could save up our money and buy really splash wardrobes this fall."

"Always thinking about clothes," Brose said.

"Well," I argued, "it'd help out a lot if I could pay for them. Then Dad would only have to take care of my tuition and board and things like that."

"And books," Brose reminded. "You'll have to do a

little studying."

"Funny boy!" I said. "But anything I earned would help out. You have to admit that."

Brose blew a loud, raucous whistle on a wide blade of grass, practically splitting my eardrums. "Somehow," he said, "I can't exactly see you working. You're just not the type."

I ruffled with resentment at his tone. "Why not?" I demanded.

"Well," Brose enumerated maddeningly, "for one thing, you're kind of lazy and for another, you don't know much that would help you get a job and—"

I broke in, glaring at him, "Why, of all the stinky things to say! I am not lazy! And I guess I know just as much as you do. If you can get a job there's no earthly reason I couldn't, too. What do you know about operating on trees?"

"Simmer down now," Brose said mildly. "I didn't mean to make you mad. I just mean—well, you do like to sleep late in the morning. And girls' jobs are different. You have to know how to type or do bookkeeping or—" he ran down.

"There are plenty of things I can do," I informed him coldly, racking my brain to think what they were. "I can —well, I can sell. I could be a salesgirl, or—or I could do filing. Anyone can do that who knows the alphabet. There are plenty of jobs I could get—just as good ones as yours, too!"

"Okay," Brose said. "Okay. Take it easy, baby. Get a job if you want to."

There was a kind of pleased gleam in his eye that I couldn't quite fathom. And I didn't like it. He looked as if—I tried to track down the reason for his half-triumphant manner—as if he'd succeeded in putting over something shrewd. But all he'd done was to hurt my feelings and imply that I wasn't smart enough or ambitious enough to get a summer job. But I'd show him I could—

Suddenly a blinding light broke over me. I stared accusingly at Brose and he had the grace to look a little disconcerted.

"Brose Gilman," I said in a low, deadly tone, "will you tell me the absolute truth about something?"

"Why, of course, Tobey," he said ingratiatingly. "I always tell you the truth, don't I?"

"Have you been needling me deliberately," I demanded, "just so I'd get mad enough to go out and find a job in order to show you I could?"

"Well, I—" Brose sort of gulped.

"Tell me!" I raised my tennis racquet threateningly. "Do you want me to get a job, too?"

Brose grinned his most beguiling grin, but I steeled myself against it. "Well," he admitted, "I can't say I exactly relish the idea of you chasing around having fun with a lot of idle guys all summer, while I work my fingers to the bone. If you get a job, too—well, I'll know where you are every day. And I'll feel easier."

Despite my effort to stop it, I felt my face begin to break into a smile. Then I started laughing. Brose joined in and we howled till we were breathless. Every time I thought of him using psychology on me, it struck me funny all over again. And apparently he was equally amused at the realization of how quickly I'd seen through his elaborate ruse.

When I could speak, I gasped, wiping my eyes with the back of my hand, "Okay, you win."

"You mean you will look for a job?" Brose asked.

I nodded. "Unless my parents won't let me."

"They'll probably be just as pleased with the idea as mine were," Brose said. "But let me warn you not to dilly-dally around too long. Lots of kids will be looking for summer jobs and they don't grow on trees, you know."

"Yours did," I said.

"Ouch!" Brose groaned.

"Anyway," I informed him, "you'll see that I can find a job if I want one. A good job, too."

"Attagirl," Brose grinned.

He got up and pulled me to my feet. "Tell you what I'll do to celebrate your imminent entry into the business world. I'll buy you a soda. Only don't go backing down on me now."

"I won't," I promised. "I'll feel my parents out tonight."

And I did.

Rather to my surprise, they seemed to think my idea of getting a summer job was a good one. I had all sorts of arguments marshaled in the back of my mind, ready to throw into the battle. But there wasn't any battle. Midge found the idea of my getting a real honest-to-goodness job so excruciatingly funny she could hardly finish her dessert. But my parents took me quite seriously, so I ignored Midge.

Dad said, his glance approving, "Now that's as sensible a notion as I've heard you come up with in a long time, Tobey."

And Mom agreed, "It certainly would help out. Everything is so high, I have been a little worried about all the clothes you're going to need for college."

"Not only clothes," Dad said. "I was getting a line from Alicia and Adam when they were home, about tuition and room and board and all." He shook his head ruefully. "All I can say is I'm glad I've only got one more daughter after Tobey to educate."

"Me?" Midge exclaimed in horror. "I don't want to go to college. All I intend to do is finish high school."

"That's what you think now," Mom told her. "But you'll feel differently later on."

Dad said, getting back to the orginal subject of the conversation, "Of course, I don't want you earning so much money I can't list you as a dependent on my income tax."

And Mom reminded him, "There's our vacation, too. Would her getting a summer job interfere with that?"

We always spend Dad's vacation at our cottage at Green Lake in July. It's a family tradition. I hadn't looked that far ahead myself. It seemed my working would cause all sorts of complications.

Dad said thoughtfully, "We could go to the lake in August instead. I've been thinking of it anyway, because business is more slack then. If Tobey got a job fairly soon she could quit early in August. That ought to work out all right."

What he said was quite reasonable. It would be better all around to work through the early part of the summer, then have a few weeks of rest and relaxation to finish off with. I felt my own enthusiasm for the whole project mounting as we discussed it. Instead of this just being a summer like every other summer, it would be special, different, exciting. It would be a summer to look back on all the rest of my life as the one when I got my first job.

I determined to start combing the want ads in the paper that very night. . . .

8

Job hunt

THE PHONE RANG JUST AS WE WERE leaving the table and I raced Midge for it, but she won. It was Barbie, so Midge handed over the phone grudgingly and went into the living room and turned on the radio real loud. Honestly, I don't know what possesses kids her age. They just love to be difficult! Dad made her turn it down, though, so I could finally hear what Barbie had to say.

I was vitally interested, because I had already told Barbie of my intention to look for a summer job. And she had been mad about the idea, too, and had promised to feel out her parents on the subject at dinner time. In fact, she and I had got so involved in our discussion of the subject, I had almost forgotten to tell her about Dick Allen enlisting, although that had been my main purpose in stopping by at her house after Brose went home. But when I did think to mention Dick, Barbie was almost as thrilled by the thought of him in uniform as I was.

Now she began, without preamble, "Tobey, they didn't object a smidgin! How about yours?"

"Mine either," I admitted. "It's all set. I'm going to start looking for a job right away in the evening paper."

"Wait for me," Barbie commanded. "I'll be right over."

She got there just as I finished drying the dishes and Barbie and I went into the living room and managed to extract the want-ad section of the Edgewood *Daily Journal* from Dad, who was reading the sports news. We took it into the library for privacy and sprawled on the floor perusing the printed columns. Under HELP WANTED—FEMALE there were several ads seeking someone to do housework or take care of babies, certainly not the sort of career on which Barbie and I were eager to embark.

"Secretary," Barbie read aloud, "over twenty, knowledge of shorthand and typing essential."

"That lets us out on three counts," I said. "Here's one for a dishwasher in Stoddards' Restaurant."

"Just what we always wanted," Barbie exclaimed glumly. "How about—no, that's for a middle-aged woman."

Doggedly we read down to the end of the column. Then our glances met in dismay. There just weren't any ads for anything we could do, or wanted to do.

"They can't do this to us!" I said abjectly.

And Barbie sighed, "Maybe this is just a bad day."

My father came in then, looking for the rest of the paper. We handed it over without argument, our faces glum.

"No luck?" Dad asked sympathetically.

Barbie and I shook our heads.

"Oh, well," Dad said, "don't give up yet. Rome wasn't built in a day, you know."

Barbie cracked, "It wasn't the construction business we wanted to get into, Mr. Heydon."

My father found this funny enough to laugh at. But I gave Barbie a reproachful look. "How corny can you get?" I inquired.

She had the grace to look slightly ashamed. She said, "Maybe it's easier for boys to get summer jobs. Sox already has one at the super market. And Brose lined up his tree-pruning deal without much trouble."

"For Perkins?" Dad asked. Then, as I nodded, he went on, "Perkins is always looking for extra help in the summer. He has more work than he can handle, so he hires a bunch of boys every year."

"Don't you know of anyone who hires a bunch of girls?" I asked hopefully.

But my father didn't.

Barbie and I concentrated on looking for jobs all that week. We answered ads that were even slightly promising, we made inquiries in every likely place we could think of, such as the dime store and the telephone company. No one seemed interested in the services of two neat, intelligent, energetic girls who merely wanted to work during summer vacation. If we had been willing to take permanent jobs, we might have found some. But temporary? Sorry, no openings.

"I'm getting tired of the whole thing," Barbie said impatiently, when nothing had turned up after several days. "Aren't you?"

I nodded, sloshing my soda around and around with a straw. It was a good soda, as all sodas were at Joe's Grill. Joe had put an extra cherry on top, too, just out of the goodness of his heart and because he liked us. We liked Joe, too. All the high-school crowd did. His restaurant and fountain were the favorite teen hangout in town. It was ten o'clock in the morning, a slightly unusual hour to be eating sundaes or hamburgers or drinking soft drinks. But even now the place was well filled with customers. Barbie and I had been lucky to find a booth to ourselves, where we could discuss our problems freely.

I said, "You don't suppose we should answer some of those ads for baby sitters? The kind where they want someone every day?"

Barbie shuddered. "I like kids okay," she said, "but not in my hair five days a week."

My sentiments exactly. I nodded. "Let's hold off a while longer anyway. Maybe something less revolting will turn up."

"Yeah, let's," Barbie agreed.

I sighed. Somehow a sort of flatness seemed to have fallen over everything since school was out. Maybe it was a natural reaction after being so rushed and busy for weeks, with all the excitement of the prom and graduation. Now there was a definite letdown. Other summers there had always been plenty to do, with Brose and Sox dropping over to suggest tennis or badminton, or a swim at the pool. Now that they both had jobs and we didn't, there were too many hours in the days. Evenings were okay, but being stymied the way we were in our job hunting was casting a definite blight on our summer. Barbie sighed, too.

A familiar male voice behind me said, "Well, if it isn't Tobey. I phoned your house and your mother said I just might find you here."

I glanced up, agreeably surprised, into Dick Allen's smiling face. "Why, Dick!" I exclaimed. "I didn't know you were home yet."

Dick nodded, greeting Barbie politely, if without any particular enthusiasm, and sat down beside me as I slid over to make room for him. "Got back yesterday," he admitted. His glance was serious for just a moment. "I won't be around too long, though. I suppose Judy told you all about it?"

"Yes, she did," I said.

"So," Dick grinned, "I'm in the navy now. In a week or so they'll be shipping me off to Great Lakes."

Barbie and I said all the usual things that people say under such circumstances. We joked and laughed, but all the time there was a little ache in the back of my throat that made my voice sound a shade husky. Why did things always have to change, I wondered? Why couldn't they just go on, simple and easy and uncomplicated, the way they used to be? Dick would be something really special in uniform. But I'd liked him fine just as he was. And while he'd been away at college most of the time and I hadn't got to see him sometimes for months on end, this would be different, altogether different.

"You'll write to me?" Dick asked, half kidding, but with an undertone of seriousness, too.

"Of course," I said, without a second's hesitation, although, like all my family, I hated writing letters and always put off even the absolutely necessary ones as long as possible. "I'll write you often and tell you all the news."

"Good," Dick grinned. "I'll need lots of letters."

We talked awhile longer. It was Barbie who happened to mention the fact that we were looking for summer jobs, so far with a notable lack of success.

"Oh?" Dick said. "What kind of jobs?"

"We're not even fussy any more," I told him ruefully. "And we long ago gave up the idea of both getting one in the same place. We're just looking for jobs, period."

Dick's tone was thoughtful. "Have you tried the super market? There's a sign in the window for a checker. I saw it just now when I passed the place."

"There is?" Barbie jumped to her feet, a wild gleam in her eye. "At the super market?" She looked at me pleadingly. "D'you mind if I rush right over, Tobey? If they need more than one I'll let you know."

"Of course," I said, and Barbie was gone in a flash.

"Well," Dick said, "I didn't mean to help her out. It was really you I had in mind."

I explained about Sox Trevor working at the super market. "That's why she's so anxious. Anyway, I wish I could get a—well, a more interesting job than that. Something—well—" I didn't know exactly how to go on.

"Yeah," Dick said, "I know. I always have a yen for that kind of a summer job, too. Something colorful, different—" he broke off with a little chuckle. "So I usually end up running a mowing machine out at the country club, or as life guard at the pool. One summer I sold magazine subscriptions."

"You won't have to think about summer jobs for a while now," I reminded him.

"Yeah," Dick said, "that's right. Join the navy and see the world, to coin a phrase. You know, Tobey," he went on, his tone a shade more serious, "it was just getting me down. All this 'will I be drafted, won't I be drafted' stuff. And if so, when and what branch will I land in? I thought, the heck with it! Joining the navy'll settle it once and for all. So now it's settled and I feel better already." He grinned ruefully, "Not a very patriotic attitude, maybe, but there it is."

"It's the way most everyone feels, I guess," I told him.

But I knew there was more to it than the things Dick

had told me. Deep things, the same strong urge to protect our country that our fathers and grandfathers had felt and that our descendants would feel, too, eventually. But they weren't the sort of things one talked about aloud without feeling flag-waving and silly. You kept them locked up inside of you and sometimes on Memorial Day at the parade, or when you sang "America, the Beautiful" or "The Star Spangled Banner" they ached in your throat and made your eyes sting.

Dick walked me home after a while. It was sheer fate that Brose should be trimming a tree on the parkway in front of the Gunderson's house as we passed by. I saw the Perkins truck and glanced up and sure enough, there he was, astride a limb of a big oak tree, staring balefully down at me through the branches.

"Oh, hi, Brose," I said somewhat lamely.

And Dick looked at me as though I'd lost my mind, until he saw Brose frowning at us from his leafy perch. Then he spoke, too, and Brose answered a trifle grudgingly.

"I see they've got you up a tree," Dick cracked.

I laughed, but Brose didn't seem to find it very funny. After a few moments of definitely stilted conversation, Dick and I walked on. After all, what else could I do? I knew Mr. Perkins wouldn't want us keeping Brose from his work. But I was sure I'd hear more on the subject from Brose—lots more!

And I did that very night. Dick had asked me to go out with him, but I already had a date with Brose, so I said no. But did Brose appreciate it? By no means. He bawled the dickens out of me as soon as we were alone in his family's car, which he had been lucky enough to wangle for the evening.

"Fine thing!" Brose griped, heading down Main Street and out toward the drive-in theater. "As soon as my back's turned, that wolf pops up and starts working on you!"

"He is *not* a wolf," I said coldly. "Dick is a real swell person. And we're good friends. Is there anything wrong in that?"

"Why doesn't he get somebody his own age?" Brose demanded.

Dick is a mere year and a half older than I am, but to hear Brose go on about it, you'd think he was thirty, at least. I glanced out the window aloofly, as though I was vitally interested in the scenery.

"Anyway," Brose growled, "I thought he was in the navy."

"He is," I said. "He'll be going up to Great Lakes almost any time."

"The sooner, the better," Brose said. But he sounded just a bit relieved. "Navy discipline will do him good."

"Why can't you like Dick?" I demanded.

"You really want to know?" Brose asked.

"Yes, I do," I informed him with dignity. "I'd like very much to know. Your attitude toward him is so childishly unreasonable."

"There's nothing childish about it," Brose said. "I'll put it very simply, in words of one syllable if possible, so you'll understand. Remember back last fall when we had a small misunderstanding just before the Heart Hop? So who took you?"

"Dick," I admitted. "But you went with Mary Andrews and—"

"Wait," Brose cut in. "I'm explaining every thing you asked me to explain—remember? So all right. So Dick took you to the Heart Hop. Then there was the little matter of that football week end at college he invited you to —and you went."

"But you were out of town," I reminded, "visiting your grandparents. And you said it would be okay."

"Not till you twisted my arm," Brose said. "But to get on—who did I have to step over every time I came to your house all during Christmas vacation?"

"He wasn't around that often," I denied, feeling a warm little glow just the same at the memory of the lovely rush I'd had between the two of them. "You're just unfair where Dick's concerned."

"And after he was home for spring vacation," Brose went on like a steam roller, "you wouldn't even wear my class ring any more."

"Brose Gilman," I exclaimed indignantly, "you know he had nothing whatever to do with that!"

"Well, maybe so," Brose admitted grudgingly, "but he could have exerted an unconscious influence over you. All that line you handed me about us being too grown up for class rings and such—that's the kind of subversive ideas you could get from associating with an older guy."

If that wasn't just like a man, blaming Dick for everything, merely because he didn't like him. I was so mad I felt like telling Brose to turn around and drive home. But the movie at the drive-in was one I particularly wanted to see. So I didn't.

But I sat half the width of the car seat away from Brose all during the first part of the picture. If it hadn't been such a romantic story and if the moon hadn't been so lovely and bright, I probably wouldn't have relaxed and got over being mad all evening. But it's awfully hard to stay angry at the drive-in. . . .

9

A worthy civic cause

I DIDN'T LOOK FOR A JOB NEARLY AS hard after Dick got home. Even the fact that Barbie was all set at the super market didn't spur me on the way it should. With Sox to put in a good word for her, she'd had an inside track. And every day she told me how grand it was to be earning money toward her college wardrobe, even though her feet did hurt from being on them so much. I listened and agreed and continued to go through the motions of looking for work. But somehow I didn't feel nearly so downhearted when nothing turned up.

The thing was, with Dick around there just seemed to be so much to do every day. We had such fun, playing tennis and going swimming and driving out into the country for picnic lunches. Brose was fit to be tied, of course, but I reminded him that Dick would only have a short time more at home. And I pointed out, too, that the least his friends could do was to make his last civilian days happy ones. Brose still didn't like it, but I managed to keep him from quite reaching the boiling point.

And then one day when I had gone into Mr. Tweedie's

real estate office mainly because Mom had called his ad to my attention, rather than because I had any real hope of anything coming of it, I got a job. Isn't that always the way? Things happen when you least expect them to, or when you're least anxious to have them happen. I think there is something fiendishly perverse about fate sometimes.

In a way, it worked out all for the best, though. Brose had begun to suspect that I wasn't really looking for a job very hard, that I was having too much fun chasing around with Dick, to bother. So when I went to work for Mr. Tweedie, it convinced Brose that he must have been doing me an injustice. And besides, Dick had to leave for Great Lakes only a few days later.

I can't deny I hated to have him go. The thought of not seeing him during all the weeks of his boot training made me feel quite sad. I kissed him good-bye on our last date. It wasn't a particularly meaningful kiss, more just the warm, friendly type, but Brose would have been furious anyway if he'd known about it.

"You're a sweet kid, Tobey," Dick told me, his arm lying along the back of the car seat behind me, his hand pressing my shoulder. "I hope I haven't messed things up too badly for you with Brose."

He knows how I feel about Brose. And he is also aware of how jealous Brose can be. Dick is very understanding. Sometimes I wish I could tell him how mixed up my feelings are about *him*. I know I like him a lot, that we always have fun together. At times it seems to me that my feelings toward Dick are the same as they might be toward an older brother, if I had one. But at other times they're not like that at all. Life can be very confusing.

I told Dick, "Brose will be okay when you're gone."

"I suppose so." Dick's grin was a little wry. He asked then, his glance direct and a bit unsettling on mine, "He's still top man, I take it?"

I could only nod, my throat aching.

"Well, all reet!" Dick's grin broadened. "Don't look so glum about it." He patted my shoulder. "So long as we stay good friends, I won't complain."

I smiled back at him. Sometimes I suspect that Dick likes things just as they are between us, nice and easy and undemanding. And then again, I'm not quite sure. . . .

With Dick away, Brose and I got along fine. My days were busy, if not too exciting, working in Mr. Tweedie's small, glass-fronted office, with the row of potted geraniums on the window ledge. My job consisted of answering the phone and writing receipts for payments and sending out notices and keeping the geraniums watered. The woman who holds the job regularly can't work in the summer when her children aren't in school. So Mr. Tweedie always hires a replacement for her till the first of August, when he closes up the office for a month and takes his own vacation. It couldn't have been a more satisfactory arrangement from my viewpoint. The pay was quite good and the work was certainly a lot easier than Barbie's. She had got used to being on her feet so much, but adding up the price of groceries all day long got a little boring. Besides, she said people were always complaining, as if it was her fault that everything was so expensive. Still, she figured she could stick it out for the summer, especially with Sox working at the same place.

Often Brose stopped by at five o'clock to walk home with me. He was getting a sensational tan with all his outdoor work and his muscles bulged impressively. He dressed for his job in jeans and high laced boots and these clothes gave him a kind of rugged appeal I found rather exciting. It seemed almost as if I were associating with some fascinating stranger instead of the Brose Gilman I had known for years. When he turned up for our regular evening dates wearing slacks and a sport jacket, I felt a little let down, and I couldn't help telling him so.

"It's as if I were dating a Northwest Mountie," I complained one night, "and he didn't wear his bright red jacket."

"Silly girl," Brose grinned. "Those boots are hot and heavy. Besides, they'd look pretty conspicuous at a party."

"I suppose so," I had to admit.

"Anyway," Brose went on, pursuing the subject still further, "I like to forget about that darned job when I'm not working at it. I've spent so much time in trees this summer, I'm beginning to feel like a sparrow. First thing you know I'll start building a nest."

I laughed. But after a minute I sobered. "You know what? None of us like our summer jobs very well. They're all pretty boring when you get right down to it. Do you suppose all jobs are like that?"

"Of course not," Brose said positively. "We're just marking time this summer, earning some money, but not working at anything we're vitally interested in. It'll be altogether different after college, when we get started in the line we've studied for."

I nodded. He was right, I suppose. But I pointed out, "I haven't even decided yet what sort of work I want to do."

"It's different for a girl," Brose answered, "unless she plans to go in for some career in a big way. You'll get married and that'll be your job." His fingers closed around mine and I felt my heart swell as he went on, his voice a little husky, "I hope you'll marry me, although it'll be a long time before we can really figure on anything."

I knew it would be a long time. I knew we were too young to decide anything so important. But it was nice to think about. It was wonderful to think about. I said, smiling, my lips sort of tremulous, "Maybe I'll take you up on that. One proposal, filed for future reference. *If* you don't change your mind."

"Don't change yours," Brose said softly. "Me, I'm the faithful type. . . ."

By the time I had worked for Mr. Tweedie a few weeks, it seemed as if I had been there forever. No longer did I get panicky taking messages on the phone, or have trouble finding things in the files. In fact, I usually had to help Mr. Tweedie locate important papers in the shambles he referred to loosely as his desk.

Mr. Tweedie was quite an interesting character, sixtyish, rather bald, and with the round, pink face and wide eyes of an utterly guileless baby. But beneath this deceptive exterior, he had the soul of a pirate and liked nothing better than to snatch the handling of a desirable piece of property right out from under the nose of some rival real-estate dealer. He had a mad taste in neckties and a weakness for mystery books. Usually he had a couple of especially gory ones stashed away in his desk drawer to read if things got dull. I read them, too. I liked Mr. Tweedie.

One day he came back from a Chamber of Commerce luncheon in a singularly dejected frame of mind. "What we need," he announced, slumping down at his desk and fixing me with an accusing look, as if it were all my fault, "is an angle. A different approach. The whole business will be a colossal flop if somebody doesn't think of some gimmick to put it over."

I knew he was talking about the Edgewood Centennial celebration, which was due to take place shortly and in which the Chamber of Commerce was taking a very active part. There would be a parade and a pageant based on the town's history. But Mr. Tweedie had long been dissatisfied with the way the whole affair was being promoted. Now he said, with a moody scowl that looked totally out of place on his cherubic countenance, "Nobody could think of anything. Call themselves a Chamber of Commerce and not one smart idea among the mouldy lot of them. Not even me," he added plaintively, as though his having let himself down was the worst blow of all.

When Mr. Tweedie sounded plaintive, I always felt an urge to pat him comfortingly on the head, as you might a child. But I restrained myself. I sat doodling idly on the pad of paper in front of me. One of my drawings turned out to look sort of like a girl in a hoop skirt. I stared at it, a vague idea nibbling at the back of my mind. Mr. Tweedie appeared about to burst into tears when I glanced up at him. I drew a ruffly parasol for my hoop-skirted lady, the idea in my mind taking more definite form.

Out of a lengthening, lugubrious silence, I suggested a trifle hesitantly, "You might have a historical tour of old houses, the way they do down in Natchez and Mobile. That would fit in."

Mr. Tweedie stared at me thoughtfully. "Old houses, hmmm," he sort of rolled the syllables around on his tongue as though he liked the sound of them. "A historical tour of old houses," he repeated. Suddenly the most beatific smile burst over his face. "What could be a more fitting adjunct to a centennial celebration than a tour of Edgewood's old houses? And how we can go to town promoting it! Now why," he demanded, "didn't I think of that?"

He proceeded to make up for his failure to do so by adopting my tentative little suggestion as though it had been his own. Not that I cared. But his enthusiasm was almost overwhelming. Mr. Tweedie leaped to his feet and paced around excitedly, throwing his arms wide in a gesture that endangered the geraniums and addressing me in ringing tones, as though I were a large audience. "A thing like that," he informed me, "would make our town richly aware of the true importance of its history, our proud local heritage and so on and so on. Besides," he beamed at me, "it'll be a fine thing for business, especially the real estate business. Old houses haven't been moving the way they should lately. This could give the market just the shot in the arm it needs. Not," Mr. Tweedie added hastily, masking the pirate gleam in his eye with narrowed lids, "that we'll be grossly commercial about it. But a historical tour of the fine old houses of Edgewood, properly publicized on a high, dignified plane, could bring in visitors from all the towns roundabout—even as far away as Chicago. City people just love an excuse to drive out into the country. And, human nature being what it is, they'll jump at the chance to snoop through some interesting old houses."

I could see just how Mr. Tweedie's mind was working. No doubt he was dreaming of getting rid of the old Porter place and the Blaine place and several others that had been a drug on the market for months now. Probably he'd do it, too, if he got enough visitors to the centennial celebration locked in the spell of the past.

"Would you have hostesses to conduct people through the houses?" I asked, remembering still more of all I'd read about such tours. "Girls in old-fashioned costumes and everything?"

Mr. Tweedie's smile widened till it threatened to hook itself over his ears. "Fine, fine!" he nodded. "We'll get some of the women's organizations in town to work up that angle. Women are so conscious of history—and such tireless workers once their enthusiasm is aroused. Mrs. Tweedie is very active in the Woman's Club. She'll know just how to go about it. And I'll see to it personally, Tobey, that you get to be a hostess or a guide or whatever, if you care to. Now I've got to call some of the Chamber of Commerce members. We'll have a special meeting. . . ."

My mother is quite active in the Woman's Club, too, so a few nights later, at dinner, I wasn't too surprised to hear her start talking about plans for a conducted tour of old Edgewood houses, to be sponsored jointly by the Woman's Club and the Chamber of Commerce in connection with the centennial.

Dad's look was so skeptically amused that Mom said, before he had a chance to open his mouth, "Now, Henry, don't start throwing cold water on the idea. You have simply no sense of the deep spiritual values inherent in any town's history."

"Just what," Dad asked, "are the spiritual values inherent in wasting time sight-seeing through some of these local mausoleums?"

"What's a moss—a mossel—what you said?" Midge asked fascinatedly, her loaded fork arrested halfway to her mouth.

But Mom didn't give Dad a chance to explain. She said indignantly, "There are some very fine examples of pure

Victorian architecture in Edgewood. The old residential section is full of them. The Hanover place and MacTavish's and Miss Tess Wentworth's—"

"Is her house," Midge interrupted, "one of those things Daddy said? Is it, Mom?"

Miss Tess is Adam Wentworth's great-aunt and we know her quite well, especially Midge, who is a particular favorite of hers. Miss Tess had Christmas Eve dinner with us last year and she loaned me my pick of the Gay Nineties clothes in her attic when I was in the school play. Maybe she'd do it again, if Mr. Tweedie made good on his promise to see that I got to be a hostess for the tour.

But suddenly, as my mother talked on, elaborating on the plan she had no idea I'd thought of, a glaring flaw in it became apparent to me. Finally I couldn't help objecting, "But, Mom, will Miss Tess and the rest of them let a bunch of strange people wander all through their houses?"

"Of course not," Dad said shortly. "The very notion's fantastic. They won't consider letting outsiders step foot in their precious old—"

My mother stopped him with a look. "For a very worthy civic cause?" she asked coolly. "Naturally we're going to charge people to go through the houses. And every owner we've approached so far has agreed as soon as they learn what we're going to use the money for."

I opened my mouth to speak and then thought better of it. Maybe if I merely listened, I'd learn in what way a plan for promoting Edgewood in order to help the real estate business was a worthy civic cause.

"Everyone," Mom went on, "knows how terribly overcrowded the hospital is. With the money we raise on this tour as a starter, other organizations are sure to get behind it and we'll have enough for a new wing in no time."

"Oh," my father nodded. "Well, that's a worthy civic cause, all right."

I didn't say anything. I felt a little bit like the boy who threw a pebble and started an avalanche. Maybe, I thought, they'd put a bronze plate on one of the doors in the new hospital wing with my name on it. But, no, they wouldn't do that, because no one knew I'd thought of the idea that grew into all this. And I wasn't going to tell, either, I thought with inner amusement. Let Mr. Tweedie take the credit. After all, he'd worked out all the angles.

10

Centennial day

It seemed to me that I ate and breathed and slept to a running crossfire of details about the historical tour of old houses during the next few weeks. Daytimes I heard them from Mr. Tweedie and evenings from Mom. The Woman's Club had jumped into the project with both feet and there must have been times when the Chamber of Commerce had a hard time trying to keep the management of it in their own hands. Or maybe they didn't care, since the Edgewood Centennial was getting so much publicity now that it was bound to be good for business, whoever was running it. Mom was so involved in club committee meetings and all, she scarcely had time to cook and take care of the house.

My sister Alicia was right in the thick of things, too. She and Adam were home from college for the summer, living with Adam's father in his big comfortable house. Mr. Wentworth co-operated in the centennial activities by having a spectacular window display in his department store. In it were all sorts of fascinating relics of the early days of the town, along with models dressed in bustles and ostrich-plumed hats and sweeping skirts, all against a background of Main Street as it had looked in the eighteen-fifties.

As Mom had predicted, most of the owners of the really old houses in town proved quite willing to throw them open to the public on Centennial Day. Not only were they anxious to help raise money toward a new hospital wing, but lots of them were members of the Woman's Club or the Chamber of Commerce, which made them even more agreeable.

Midge fixed things up with Miss Tess Wentworth before Mom even had a chance to call on her officially.

"Sure, she said okay," Midge informed us. "First she had a couple of objections, but I straightened those out. She was kind of worried about the idea of a lot of strangers traipsing through her house, but I said Tobey and Alicia could be hostesses and show people through, so that suited her fine. And then she got to wondering how she could keep out of sight during the tours, so I invited her over here to our house to spend the day. She liked that. She had such fun here Christmas." Midge asked Mom belatedly then, "That was okay, wasn't it?"

"Of course," Mom told her with a little smile. "I'll drop over and see Miss Tess right away and second your invitation."

Miss Tess proved very generous in letting centennial hostesses borrow some of the lovely old clothes in her attic. Alicia and I got first choice, of course. I picked a devastating lilac-colored silk from Miss Tess' inexhaustible collection and Alicia decided on a yellow-sprigged voile. We modeled them for Miss Tess and her eyes got all misty with memories, as she told us about the occasions they had been purchased for, years and years ago. Then she gave us tea out of fragile Haviland cups and yummy little cookies on an old silver platter. Midge sat on the floor at Miss Tess' feet and every now and then the old lady would lay an affectionate hand on her sandy head. It was all easy and friendly and quite enjoyable, despite the difference in our ages, which ranged from eleven to eighty or so. I couldn't help remembering how scared Alicia used to be of Miss Tess before Alicia and Adam were married and how mad she got at her the time she gave them the grandfather's clock for a wedding gift because she didn't understand about their going to live in a quonset at college. Miss Tess has certainly mellowed since those days, or else it's just that we all treat her more like a human being now and realize how lonely she gets living all alone in her great gingerbready house. At any rate, she gets along fine with all of us and she kept telling us how she was looking forward to spending Centennial Day at our house and watching the parade from our front porch and all.

"It's so sweet of you to have me, when you're all going to be so busy," she remarked, her white head held high, but her smile a little doubtful, as though she weren't quite sure she wouldn't be in our way.

"We're looking forward to having you," I told her.

And Alicia said, "Of course, we are. And Tobey and I will take good care of your house, too, and see that nothing gets hurt or disturbed."

We went on to explain to her how the rooms would be roped off, so that the visitors could just walk along the halls and look through the doorways. And Miss Tess nodded and agreed and seemed to be getting a big bang out of the whole thing. I expect, when you're eighty, any change from your regular routine seems pretty exciting.

All our crowd was involved in the centennial doings to

some extent. Brose was driving one of the old carriages in the parade. He was going to wear tight trousers, a tail coat and a high beaver hat, so he'd be in keeping with the girls in old-fashioned costumes who would ride with him. Lots of ancient vehicles had been unearthed from dusty stables and cleaned and polished for the occasion. Barbie was one of the drum majorettes marching with the band. And Sox Trevor and Itchy Stearns, in costumes as resplendent as Brose's, were to ride on a pair of antique bicycles, the kind with one enormous wheel and one tiny one. We had laughed at them, rehearsing, till we cried.

Everyone who had old equipment or clothing had loaned it for the occasion. Centennial Day was truly a town project. And cars full of interested visitors began to arrive early in the morning and the flow continued all day. Never had Edgewood's parking problem been so acute, never had our streets been thronged with so many strangers. They lined both sides of Main Street as the parade moved along through alternating stretches of hot summer sunshine and welcome patches of shade. Several of us girls who were riding with Brose in the fringed-top surrey had coquettish little parasols and we found they were very handy for keeping the sun out of our eyes.

I caught a glimpse of a whole crowd of people, with Miss Tess and Adam's father in the midst of them, viewing the parade from the vantage point of our porch, which happened to be on the line of march. The morning was gay and sort of electric with all the people milling about and the brisk sharpness of the band music and the clack of horses' hooves on the pavement and voices shouting greetings from all sides.

Afterwards Alicia and I hurried over to Miss Tess' house and found that a crowd of people was already gathering in front of it, eager to get in. It was the first house listed for the tour and people were reading about it in the guidebook they had received with their tickets. This told of the house being built by Miss Tess' father, back in 1870 or so. There were lots of interesting historical details about it, too, such as the fact that King Edward of England, then the Prince of Wales, had attended a party in the ballroom on the third floor when he was visiting in America during the Gay Nineties.

"I didn't even know the house had a ballroom," I confided to Alicia, as I skimmed hastily through the guidebook.

"It's got everything," Alicia said. "I haven't seen half the rooms myself. Adam says there are more than twenty."

"Do you suppose," I asked then, dreamily, "that Miss Tess danced with the Prince?"

"It's hard to imagine her dancing," Alicia said with a little laugh, "but I suppose she must have."

We didn't have much chance to talk, once the crowd started coming in. We were kept busy all day long, escorting one group after another along the dim old halls, pointing out interesting features of the various rooms beyond the ropes, answering questions and trying to keep children from sliding down the wide polished banister of the curving stairs. I could sympathize more than ever with Barbie now. My feet were tired before noon and along toward four o'clock, when the tour was scheduled to close officially, they were killing me. The tight-waisted bodice of my lilac silk dress seemed to grow more stifling by the minute. I guess girls used to be more wasp waisted than we moderns are. I felt sticky and cross as the last group of visitors assembled for their tour of the house.

Alicia led the way and I brought up the rear as we started

on our final trip. Trial and error had taught us that this was the most effective method. Otherwise, if we both went ahead, we were likely to lose some stragglers and have to go back for them. There were several children with this group and I kept having to stop them from slipping under the ropes and into the rooms to investigate Miss Tess' fascinating collection of bric-a-brac at closer range. My temper grew shorter by the minute, but I curbed it. I answered questions politely and with a slightly strained smile on my weary face. Finally, as we were on the last lap of our trip, I began to relax. Alicia was preceding the party down the curving stairway, I was limping along behind, when one small angelic-looking demon of about six eluded my vigilance and his mother's somewhat sketchy attention, and leaped onto the banister like a horse-opera hero mounting his steed. Before I could put out a hand to stop him, he was swooping downward, yelling gleefully, passing one startled person after another who was taking the more customary means of descending stairs. With supreme presence of mind, Alicia caught him just as he hit the round, ornately carved ball that topped the newel post. He wasn't hurt at all and he proceeded to squirm out of her clutch and insert his hand trustingly into his mother's. She did nothing more drastic than to admonish her little darling, "Why, dear, you shouldn't have done that," and give Alicia and me a vaguely apologetic smile.

As I reached the foot of the stairs, I noticed that the ball top of the newel post had been knocked loose by the impact. It hung crookedly sideways and I was appalled by this damage to Miss Tess' property. Alicia was conducting the party on through the door, so I paused to see if I could straighten the carved piece of mahogany. To my horror, it came off in my hands and I stood staring stupidly down into what appeared to be a small compartment in the top of the newel post. And in the compartment was a letter, slightly yellowed with age, addressed simply in a bold, masculine hand, "Tess." Gingerly shifting the carved ball to one hand, I reached out and lifted the thin envelope, turned it in my fingers. It was sealed.

I stood there, frowning perplexedly down at it, until I heard the sound of Alicia's footsteps coming back across the front porch. What impulse moved me then, I'll never know. But some urge, too strong to resist, impelled me to put the faded envelope back hastily into its hiding place and settle the wooden ball firmly back where it belonged. I found that by turning it a little it was once more fixed firmly and apparently immovably in place.

"Well," said Alicia with a deep sigh of relief, "that's over. I thought we'd never get rid of that last batch, didn't you?"

I nodded, feeling queerly unsettled and disturbed, but not quite wanting to tell Alicia of my mysterious discovery. Somehow it seemed as if the old letter in the newel post was a secret of Miss Tess' that I was compelled to keep, even from my sister.

"What's the matter, Tobey?" Alicia asked frowning. "You look so queer."

"I—guess it's just the heat," I gulped, managing a smile. "And this dress is getting tighter every second."

"Mine, too," Alicia admitted. "And then that little brat sliding down the banister startled me about out of my hide."

"Didn't he, though?" I agreed.

Brose rang the doorbell then. "Hurry and let's lock up the joint," he said when I opened the door for him. "I'm supposed to drive you two home in a hurry, your mother says, so you can get out of those museum clothes and into something cool before supper."

I grinned at him. "You're good news," I said. "I've never been hotter or hungrier in my life. Just a sandwich for lunch and these clothes are beginning to feel like a suit of armor."

I looked enviously at his light slacks and loud-printed sport shirt. And Brose gave me a little hug and said, "There's nothing wrong with you that a shower and your mother's buffet supper won't cure, is there? You have to be in shape to enjoy the pageant tonight."

"Thank goodness we'll only be onlookers at that," Alicia said fervently. "Personally, I'll take the twentieth century."

When we got home and showered and put on cool dresses, we began to feel practically human again. Supper was salady and delicious on our big screened porch. Mom and Dad had a whole crowd of people over and we were all very gay and informal. Miss Tess held court vivaciously from a comfortable wicker chair and everyone listened to what she had to say and lavished all kinds of attention on her.

"She's such a dear," I murmured to Brose, who was perched on the arm of my chair. "I'll bet she was quite a belle in her day."

"Yeah," Brose nodded. "I wonder why she never married?"

"I've wondered about that, too," I admitted. "According to that big portrait of her over her mantel, she was really beautiful when she was young."

"And with all that moola, too," Brose cracked.

The memory of the yellowed letter in the mahogany newel post was sharp suddenly in my mind. Why had Miss

Tess hidden it there, I wondered, and left it so many years? As my thoughts nibbled away at the problem, a startling fact occurred to me, one I had been aware of before, but which hadn't struck me as important.

The letter was sealed.

Now, recalling that inconsistency, I frowned. And Brose's voice went on, saying words I didn't hear at all.

I thought: But if Miss Tess never opened it, how could she know what the letter said? And why would anyone hide away an unread letter?

All that evening I kept pondering various questions about my accidental discovery. I'm afraid I didn't pay too much attention to the pageant of Edgewood's history, which was given in the park. It all went off very well and the night was lovely, clear and moonlit. Sitting close beside Brose in the pleasant darkness, feeling his hand on mine, I tried to dismiss the troubling memory of Miss Tess' letter. After all, it was no business of mine. If some strange little brat hadn't chosen to take a slide down her banister, I'd never even have known of the letter's existence. And if Miss Tess hid unopened letters away in secret places—well, that was her own affair. Why was I worrying about it?

"Tobey!" Brose's repeated insistent whisper finally penetrated my abstraction. "What's wrong with you?"

"Why—nothing," I murmured. "Just watching the pageant."

"Like heck you are," Brose growled. "You're a million miles away from here and from me. And I don't like it."

"Okay." I leaned my shoulder chummily against his. "I'm back now. I guess spending the day in that old house and in those old-fashioned clothes cast a sort of spell over me."

Brose's lips whispering, almost against my ear, "I'm the one who's suppose to cast a spell over you, baby," finally made me forget about the letter.

At least, for the time being. . . .

11

The letter

EVERYONE WAS PLEASED WITH THE Edgewood Centennial and its results. The Chamber of Commerce felt it had been a fine thing for the town. The Woman's Club was proud of the amount of money that had been raised toward a new hospital wing. All the other participating organizations felt the project had been a worth-while effort. And Mr. Tweedie succeeded in selling the old Porter house, which had been a drug on the real-estate market for years, to an insurance outfit which was anxious to move its headquarters out of Chicago and into a smaller community.

"If it hadn't been for the publicity we got in the city papers, they'd probably never have known Edgewood existed," Mr. Tweedie assured me earnestly. "Never underestimate the power of the press, Tobey. We'll probably sell a lot more old houses before we're through."

"That'll be fine," I said.

Mr. Tweedie opened his desk drawer and I thought he was probably getting out his newest mystery book to read. But instead he brought out a small white box and sat there, beaming at me, as he turned it back and forth in his fingers. "A lot of our publicity," Mr. Tweedie proclaimed, "was due to the historical tour of old houses. And don't think for a minute I've forgotten who thought that up. And so as a small token of my appreciation and so on and so on," he reached out and handed the little box to me, "I want to give you this. The commission on the Porter house," he admitted confidentially, "was an unusually juicy one, due to the fact that the Porters have been trying to dump—I mean sell the old barn for years."

"Why—why, thanks," I said in genuine surprise. "But you didn't have to get me anything." I started opening the package.

"Of course not," he nodded his pink bald head up and down. "But I wanted to. Appreciation where appreciation is due, that's my motto. And—who knows?—you might have another bright idea sometime and I'd like to be the one you tell it to."

I had the paper off the little box now and, as I lifted the lid, my eyes widened at sight of a lovely costume jewelry set consisting of a necklace and bracelet in silver and pearls. "Why, Mr. Tweedie," I exclaimed, "it's beautiful!"

"Glad you like it," he smiled. "I know nothing about such things myself, but Mrs. Tweedie selected it. One woman ought to know what another one would like, way I figured."

I thanked him again. The phone rang then and we proceeded to get on with the day's work. But every now and then I thought of the lovely gift in my desk drawer. This would teach me not to jump to conclusions about not being appreciated, I guessed. Here I had thought Mr. Tweedie was going to forget I'd been the one to suggest the historical tour idea. But he hadn't at all. Human nature, I decided, wasn't really as low as people were prone to think. And there was a nice warm glow in the realization. . . .

During the days that followed, the memory of the hidden letter arose every now and then to haunt me. Alicia had taken our old-fashioned clothes back to Miss Tess after the centennial, so I hadn't seen the old lady at all since that evening at our house. I really tried to dismiss the whole matter from my mind, but it's queer how an unsolved mystery like that won't stay buried, however many thoughts and impressions pour into your mind on top of it. Finally, I decided to confide the whole thing to my mother and see what she suggested.

I told her all about it one night after dinner when we were doing the dishes together. My father was listening to a news broadcast in the living room and Midge had gone out to play with Judy Allen, so we had the kitchen all to ourselves. The familiar rattle of silver and dishes, the rush of water from the faucets, made a rather unsuitable accompaniment to my strange story. Mom asked a question now and then, obviously interested, a little frown of concentration between her eyebrows.

"And it hadn't been mailed?" she turned an inquiring glance toward me. "You're sure of that?"

I shook my head. "It didn't have a stamp on it, or anything. It wasn't even addressed except just her name, just her first name," I explained. "Do you get it, Mom? Doesn't it seem awfully queer to you?"

Mom nodded. "Especially the part about it's being sealed. I don't understand that at all. Anyone might put a letter away in a secret place, an important letter, one she wanted to keep. But not," Mom's frown deepened, "without opening it, not without knowing what it said. Tobey, you don't suppose someone else could have put it there for her and Miss Tess never have known about it?"

"I don't know," I admitted. "I can't understand it at all. I suppose that's why it's troubled me ever since I happened on it. Surely, having lived in the house all her life, Miss Tess must know about the newel post having that compartment in it."

Mom nodded again, washing a dish over and over absently. "It does seem so—and yet—well, it's all very strange."

"You can say that again," I agreed. "I wish I'd never seen the darn' letter or that I could forget it. But I can't. Mom," I asked solemnly, "do you think I should tell her about it?"

My mother considered for a long moment. And then she said, her voice firm, "I really think you should, dear. It's all so odd. If you just tell her you saw it and that it's been troubling you—well, she can't take exception to that if she does know about the letter. And if she doesn't, I should think she'd be grateful. Why don't you drop over there tonight, Tobey, and get it off your mind?"

I was glad Mom felt that way about it, because I had come to the same conclusion, even if it did mean sticking my nose into something that didn't concern me. I wouldn't feel right, I knew, until I'd mentioned the letter to Miss Tess.

I asked Dad if I could use the car for a little while to do an errand. He didn't mind, so I went out to the garage and backed it out onto the street. Just as I started to swing away from the curb, I saw Brose loping up. Honestly, his sense of timing is sensational—wrong timing, that is.

Without waiting for an invitation, he climbed in beside me and sat there, beaming. "Where we going?" he inquired.

"*I*," my tone underlined the word, "have to go over to Miss Tess Wentworth's for a little while. Did we have a date?"

"Don't be like that," Brose said. "Don't you like to have me drop in unexpectedly?"

I couldn't help smiling at him. "Sure, I do," I admitted. "But I do have to see Miss Tess. I told Mom I would."

This would implant the idea in his mind that I was doing an errand for my mother and forestall any questioning on his part as to why I wanted to see Miss Tess.

"It won't take long, will it?" Brose asked hopefully. "Can't I ride along and wait for you in the car? Then we can stop at Joe's for a soda or something."

"Okay," I agreed. "You've bribed me."

We drove the few blocks to the old Wentworth house and I left Brose in the car on the curving drive. "I shouldn't be more than fifteen or twenty minutes," I told him.

"Good," Brose said, switching on the radio. "This place gives me the jumps. I shouldn't be surprised if it's haunted."

I went up the broad old steps and crossed the porch, my footsteps echoing hollowly. Miss Tess' housekeeper answered my ring. Mrs. Fairchild was a plump elderly woman with a dour, forbidding face, but she smiled faintly at the sight of me. "Why, Miss Tobey," she said in surprise. "Won't you come in?"

Miss Tess called to me from the drawing room, where I found her sitting comfortably in a rocking chair, watching television. This was a comparatively new occupation for Miss Tess and she got quite a bang out of it. But now she welcomed me graciously and asked Mrs. Fairchild to switch off the television on her way out.

"This is a pleasant surprise," she said, smiling at me. "I seldom have visitors in the evening."

"I can't stay very long," I explained, diffidence making my voice sound a little unnatural, even to my own ears. "Brose Gilman is waiting for me out in the car."

"Why, have him come in," Miss Tess suggested. "I'd be very pleased to see him."

I said apologetically, "I'd rather not, Miss Tess. You see, I came tonight for a sort of strange reason, something I want to talk to you about, to tell you—" my voice quavered.

She leaned forward a little in her chair, her bright old eyes kind and understanding. "Of course, my dear. What is it?"

I swallowed and tried to go on, but it wasn't an easy thing to find words for. She might be resentful, feel I was prying into things that didn't concern me. It had all seemed right and natural when Mom and I discussed it. But now in the shadowy, formal room, with its crimson silk drapes drawn against the night, with the lovely smiling portrait of Miss Tess when she was a girl looking down at me, I found myself gulping and coloring.

A little smile, very like that of the girl in the portrait, curved Miss Tess' thin old lips. She reached out and laid a blue-veined hand on my knee comfortingly. "Is it about the other day when you were showing people through the house?" she asked gently. And then, at my nod, "Did something get broken, some piece of bric-a-brac? Because if that's it, don't give it another thought, my dear. I have so many—"

I shook my head, interrupting, "It's not that. Nothing was broken, really. It was just that the top of the newel post came off." I went on then, finding it a little easier once I had started, and spilled out the whole story. As I talked, the little smile on Miss Tess' face faded and a look of utter disbelief came into her eyes. She stared at me, frowning, her lips slightly parted, when I had finished.

Then she asked carefully, as though weighing each word before she spoke it, "You say—there is a letter—in the newel post? Addressed to me—and still sealed?"

I nodded. "That's what bothered me, the fact that it was sealed. I was afraid—maybe—you didn't know it was there."

Miss Tess' bright, intense glance left my face and fixed itself on the portrait above the mantel, seeming to seek some answer from the image of herself as she had been more than half a century before. Then she passed a hand unsteadily across her eyes, as if to wipe away some dimness, some lack of understanding. Finally her glance came back to me.

"Will you get it?" Her voice was only a breath above a whisper. "Will you bring it to me—the letter?"

"Of course." My step was soundless on the thick carpeting with its old-fashioned pattern of lush roses. As I lifted the carved ball that topped the newel post, the whole house seemed to wait in expectant silence for what I would find there, just as Miss Tess waited behind me in the drawing room. For one fantastic second, it seemed to me that the letter would not be there, that I had dreamed the whole thing. But I hadn't. The square, yellowed envelope was thin and real in my fingers, the "Tess" scrawled across its face as stark and startling as before. I set the top of the newel post in place and retraced my steps to where Miss

Tess waited for me, her eyes fixed unwaveringly now on the letter in my hand. As I gave it to her, the old fingers clutched it tightly, eagerly, turned it over and back again as though assuring themselves that it was real.

"You—didn't know about it?" I asked wonderingly.

Miss Tess said, very low, "I didn't know." She opened her lips as though to say something further, then closed them again. Her eyes lifted pleadingly to mine and there was no misunderstanding their urgent message.

I murmured, getting to my feet. "I'll have to go now. Brose is waiting."

Miss Tess nodded. She spoke no word to deter me. Never had I seen anyone more anxious to be alone.

"You're sure you'll be all right?" I couldn't help asking.

"I'll be all right," Miss Tess smiled faintly. "And thank you, Tobey. I'm more grateful to you than you'll ever know. You've done me a very great favor tonight."

When I had said good-bye and let myself quietly out into the darkness, the sense of strangeness still hung over me like a fog. How oddly Miss Tess had acted. She hadn't known of the letter, yet she had welcomed its appearance as though she had expected it. Far from solving the mystery, my visit only served to deepen it, so far as I was concerned. And I'd probably never know the answer to the curious set of circumstances my accidental discovery had set in motion. This wasn't like a book, where you could take a surreptitious peek at the final chapter. I was as completely in the dark as ever, and likely to remain so.

I came back to the present with a dull thud at the sound of Brose's voice saying, "Well, step on it! Don't just stand there as if you're in a trance."

"Oh," I murmured vaguely. "I forgot all about you."

"Gee, thanks," Brose said, with elaborate sarcasm, opening the car door for me. "You sure took long enough. Must have been quite an errand your mother sent you on."

I didn't correct him. It was simpler to let him go on thinking that was why I had come. Instead I said thoughtfully, "I wonder how it feels to be so old, to have almost your whole life behind you?"

Brose shrugged philosophically. "I wouldn't know yet. But I'll tell you later on, if I live long enough. Frankly, though, I doubt I'll last till I'm eighty unless I get something to eat pretty quick. I'm starved."

"Me, too," I admitted, turning on the ignition.

There was no point in brooding further over Miss Tess and her mysterious letter. I had done what I felt I should and she had been grateful. Now, surely, I ought to be able to dismiss the whole matter from my mind. A double chocolate sundae with marshmallow and nuts at Joe's Grill would be a logical first step in the direction of forgetting.

12

A story from the past

Dick Allen and I had been writing quite regularly, so I knew that his period of boot training was almost over. But so many things had been happening, I'd lost track of the exact date of his first twenty-four hour leave. Judy's and Midge's excited conversation on the subject set me straight Saturday morning. Then, at noon there was a special delivery letter from Dick, telling me that he was looking forward to seeing me sometime during the evening, although, of course, his folks would expect him to spend the greater part of his short leave with them. "But there will be other leaves," Dick wrote, "when we can have real honest-to-goodness dates—that is if you still feel like wasting time on me. And how I hope you do!"

It was with some misgivings that I told Brose about Dick's impending return. After all, we had a date that night, just as we did every Saturday, and while I wouldn't have dreamed of breaking it, I thought maybe we could figure something out.

"Such as what?" Brose asked coldly. "That we should

all go out together, cozy and threesome-ish? Nothing doing!"

"I didn't mean anything like that," I denied. "It's just —well, Dick probably won't get a chance to stay over here very long. His family will want to monopolize most of his time."

"Why not all of it?" Brose inquired. "Seems to me it's his duty to stay home."

I ignored this. "Why don't you just come over here instead of our going out anywhere? We didn't really have anything special in mind. Then I'll be here when Dick comes. And, after all, isn't that only simple friendship?"

"I can think of a couple of other names for it," Brose said darkly. "Who does he think he's muscling in on, anyway? Can't he find a girl of his own and leave mine alone?" He said much more, all in the same resentful vein.

When he paused for breath, I suggested meekly, turning my most beguiling glance on him, "Why can't I ask Barbie and Sox to come over, too? Then the four of us could play some bridge or something till Dick comes. And after he goes, we could drive out for something to eat. We often spend an evening like that, you know we do, Brose. And Dick's being here for a little while won't really make much difference."

"It will to me," Brose said, scowling.

"Please?" I coaxed, slipping my hand into his.

Brose sighed. "Oh, all right," he said grudgingly.

I felt a little ashamed of myself for using my feminine wiles to get around him. But, after all, I couldn't very well just go out with him and ignore Dick completely. It wouldn't be friendly or patriotic or anything.

When I explained it all to Barbie she thought I had

taken the only possible course. And that night she and Sox came over and played a few rubbers of bridge with Brose and me on our porch. Afterward, we just sat around, drinking Cokes and gabbing about everything under the sun, as we so often do. It it hadn't been for the threat of Dick's visit hanging over Brose, I'm sure he'd have enjoyed himself.

But tonight Brose was edgy and hard to get along with. When Dick finally arrived, looking so trim and handsome in his blue uniform and perky little white cap that he almost took my breath away, Brose shook hands with him, but his manner was far from cordial. I was glad the others were there to supply a restraining influence and keep the situation from growing too explosive.

We asked a lot of questions and Dick told us quite a bit about the training camp and navy routine. It was very interesting and I could have socked Brose for his attitude of supreme boredom and the pointed way he kept yawning.

Barbie gave me sympathetic looks and tried hard to keep the conversation gay and effervescent. But Sox took his cue from Brose and contributed practically nothing to the talk. If Dick noticed any strain in the air, he gave no indication of it. He is so poised and sure of himself, so much the master of any situation. Brose didn't show up very well by comparison. And yet, in spite of my annoyance with him, I found myself feeling a surge of sympathy toward him, too. After all, it was only natural for him to be jealous. I'd been writing Dick steadily since he'd been away and I'd spent a lot of time with him during his last weeks at home. No wonder Brose felt hurt and resentful.

I did all I could to draw him into the conversation, to show him I was just as interested in him as in Dick. But

Brose was too contrary to meet me even a quarter of the way. His expression grew more and more glum and every remark he made sounded like a growl.

Dick didn't stay very long. I went with him to the door, which was only common politeness, but as we left the porch I could feel Brose's angry glance boring into my back.

When we were out of hearing distance in the front hall, Dick said, with a little chuckle, "If looks could cut throats, I'd be bleeding all over your carpet."

I found myself flying instinctively to Brose's defense. "I guess you can't really blame him. We had a date tonight."

"And I messed it up?" Dick's tone was quizzical.

"No, of course not," I said rather unhappily. "But I suppose from his viewpoint it seems that way."

Dick grinned and gave my hand a squeeze. He can be very sweet and understanding. "Can't say I blame him," he admitted. "I'd feel the same in his shoes." He asked then, "If I let you know about my next pass before you're tied up with Brose, can we have a real date?"

I knew Brose would be furious if I agreed. But, after all, I liked Dick, too. And Brose and I weren't going steady. My parents had turned thumbs down on that away back when I was wearing his class ring. Besides, Dick wasn't easy to resist, smiling down at me so hopefully, his fingers close and warm and strong around mine.

"I—guess so," I told him. . . .

When I got back to the porch Brose was pacing up and down like a lion in the zoo. "Seven minutes that took," he informed me irately, consulting his wrist watch. "How come?"

Barbie kidded, "I'll bet you've taken longer than that to say good night lots of times."

Brose glared at her. I appreciated her good intentions, but she simply didn't know how to handle him. Long practice had made me fairly adept at it. But it certainly took all my ingenuity to get around him that night. By the time we had driven down to Joe's and consumed a couple of hamburgers and a malted apiece, my sweetly attentive manner had begun to undermine Brose's grumpiness. And before the evening was over, he was practically himself again. But all in all, it wasn't an experience I'd want to live through very often. . . .

Not long after the week end of Dick's leave Midge told me, "Miss Tess says she'd like for you to stop by and see her."

My little sister's manner was frankly speculative, but I had no intention of satisfying her curiosity as to what Miss Tess might want to see me about. Besides, I wasn't sure it had anything to do with the letter in the newel post. But I hoped she might be going to shed some light on that mystery, which still rose up quite often to haunt my thoughts.

"When does she want me to come?" I asked Midge, sounding as casual as possible.

"Any time you can," Midge informed me. "She just told me this aft when I stopped in to see her on my way home from the library. What d'you s'pose she wants with you, Tobey?"

I shrugged. "If she didn't tell you, how would I know?"

This seemed to strike my little sister as reasonable. At least, she didn't ask any more questions, for which I was grateful. But my own curiosity drove me to the old Wentworth house the very next afternoon. It was Wednesday, and most of Edgewood's business offices close on Wednesday afternoons. Both Brose and Barbie have to work, though, so usually I just spend my free time washing my hair and catching up on my reading and lazing around generally.

But today was different. A queer sort of excitement kept me all stirred up as I dressed after my shower. Miss Tess is such a formal sort of person, I found myself selecting my blue pique dress and flat-heeled, white sandals and brushing my hair as carefully as though I were going to a party. I was glad that Midge was at the pool with Judy Allen and Mom had gone to a bridge luncheon. There was no one to remark about my getting so dressed up, or to ask questions. When the phone rang just as I was going out the door and I got involved in a long, rather rambling conversation with my sister Alicia, I felt as fuming and impatient as though I were being held up on my way out on a date.

But I finally escaped Alicia and got under way. When I rang Miss Tess' old-fashioned doorbell and heard it tinkling faintly away off somewhere in the depths of the house, the excitement and curiosity within me had built up to a point where my blood actually throbbed in my ears and my heart beat quickly.

This is silly, I told myself. But it didn't do any good.

Mrs. Fairchild let me in after a rather longish wait. She greeted me and explained, "I'm just gettin' Miss Tess' tea ready. You go on in the drawing room while I pop back to the kitchen before the toast burns."

Miss Tess, looking her usual regal self in something soft and lavender, welcomed me warmly. "Tobey, my dear," she said, holding both my hands for a minute in hers, "it was sweet of you to come. You must have tea with me."

I sat down opposite her and we talked casually as we waited. The big, high-ceilinged room, so full of furniture and bric-a-brac and pictures, seemed yet uncrowded and possessed of a kind of stiff Victorian charm. It and Miss Tess were perfectly at ease with each other, like old friends. As indeed they should be, I thought. Miss Tess had been born in this house, had grown old here. The family portraits ranged around the walls in their ornate frames were real people to her, not just queer old-fashioned reproductions of faces long since gone. My glance lingered on first one and then another until the housekeeper brought in tea and thin triangles of cinnamon toast and little chocolate cookies. Miss Tess remembered that I liked lemon without asking. She handed me the fragile gold-banded cup with its pattern of pink roses, and she pressed toast and cookies upon me.

Mrs. Fairchild said from the doorway as she went out, "I'm goin' over to the Davises for a bit, if you won't be needin' me. Hallie's got one of her bad migraines."

"Of course, Amelia." Did I imagine the faint note of relief in Miss Tess' voice? "You go right along."

So then we had the big house entirely to ourselves. But still our talk was casual over the delicate clink of our teacups, almost stilted it seemed to me. I found my glance wandering among the portraits again, coming to rest at last on the lovely almost life-size painting of Miss Tess over the marble mantel.

Her gaze must have followed mine. She said, her voice curiously gentle, "I was just about your age when that was painted, Tobey."

I nodded. It wasn't easy to imagine Miss Tess my age. I said and meant it, "You were so beautiful."

"Eighteen is a beautiful age." Miss Tess' tone was a little sad. "Beautiful and too soon over. Being in love imparts the semblance of beauty, too. And I was in love when that portrait was painted. I was in love with the man who painted it."

His name, I learned as Miss Tess talked on, had been Julian Millay. And he had been in his thirties. "Almost twice my age," Miss Tess admitted, "which was only one of the many reasons Papa didn't approve of him at all. Oh, he liked Julian well enough at first and he admired his work immensely. That was why he had him come here from New York to paint my portrait."

As her low voice went on, unfolding the old story, telling me things she had probably never confided to another living soul, it seemed as if I were back there with her in the faraway days of her youth. And the things she spoke of hurt me just as much as if they had happened yesterday instead of years and years before. My throat ached and I felt tears prick against my eyelids as she told how she and Julian Millay had fallen in love during the weeks he stayed here in her father's house, working on her portrait.

"At first Papa had no idea of what had happened," Miss Tess said. "But love isn't easily kept hidden. Something in our eyes, our manner, gave us away finally. And then my father, hoping to keep things from coming to a head, never left us alone together. He would sit with us while Julian painted me, he scarcely let me out of his sight except when I retired at night. He even had one of the servants spying on me. That," she admitted, "was how he must have learned of the notes Julian and I left for each other in the inner compartment of the newel post."

Now I found myself listening even more intently, seeing dimly the link with the present, realizing why she was telling me all this. We had long since set our teacups aside and now I leaned forward a little in my chair, so as to miss no word, no inflection. She and Julian had planned finally to elope, Miss Tess explained. When he left Edgewood to go back to the city, she would go with him and they would be married.

"He wasn't sure it was the wise thing." A sad little smile touched her lips. "There was the difference in our ages, the fact that I had a great deal more money than he—or would have unless Papa disinherited me. Julian said that to marry me would make him appear truly to be the fortune hunter Papa considered him. But we loved each other. And I was sure enough for both of us."

During one of their snatched seconds of privacy, Julian promised to leave a note in the newel post telling Miss Tess where to meet him the night of his departure. But he begged her to search her heart and said that if any doubts remained as to the wisdom of their course, she should simply not meet him at the appointed place and he would understand.

"As soon as I could after he had gone," Miss Tess told me, "I looked in our hiding place. There was no note there. I won't—" her voice was momentarily unsteady, "burden you with my feelings, my dear. All I could decide, when I was capable of thinking at all, was that Julian had been the one who found too many doubts in his heart, that he hadn't cared for me enough to take me with him."

She sat there, silent then, an old, old lady in the afternoon sunlight slanting in at the windows. But the hurt of the tragedy she remembered was very real in the room with us.

Impulsively I reached out and laid my hand over hers.

13

The coming of Clarissa

MOST OF THE REST OF MISS TESS' STORY was conjecture, but there seemed no reason to doubt her guess as to what must have happened. She knew her father's character, she was aware of the things of which he would have been capable, incredible as they seemed to me.

"He took the note as soon as the servant told him it had been left there," Miss Tess said positively, but without bitterness. "He would feel it was his duty, Papa would, to save me—how often I've heard him say the very words!—from my own youthful folly. But he was an honorable man in his way. He wouldn't open a letter addressed to someone else. He must have kept it locked away somewhere for years, while he paraded one eligible young man after another before me, hoping I'd fall in love with someone he considered more suitable. But I never did," Miss Tess said softly. "And perhaps Julian didn't forget me, either. The newspaper accounts of his death in Paris years ago mentioned that he had never married."

I felt a tear plop against my hand. It was the first I realized I was crying. Miss Tess' eyes were suspiciously bright, too. "But—how did the letter get back there?" I choked.

"Don't cry, my dear," Miss Tess said gently. "There's nothing to cry about now, all these years later. I wouldn't have troubled you with the story at all, except that you played a part in the final act, so is seemed you had a right to hear the beginning. My father," she explained, "no doubt returned the letter to its hiding place when he grew very old. Perhaps it weighed more heavily on his conscience as time went on. Perhaps by putting it back he lessened in his own mind the stigma of having taken it. Who knows?" Miss Tess' thin, surprisingly straight shoulders lifted in the tiniest of shrugs. "Whatever his reasons, he returned the letter to the place where he had found it. And it might have lain there indefinitely if it hadn't been for you."

"But—are you glad I found it?" I asked doubtfully. "Wouldn't you rather it had all been left shut away in the past?"

Miss Tess shook her white head firmly in the negative. "I know now," she said, "that Julian loved me, as I loved him. There were only a couple of lines in the note, just a mentioned meeting place, but he signed it, 'With all my love.' Do you imagine I wouldn't want to know that the letter existed?"

"Of course not," I said softly, around the lump in my throat.

And there seemed little more I could say. I was glad when the housekeeper came in a few minutes later to gather up the tea tray. Murmuring something vague about having to leave, I got to my feet. But there was such warmth in Miss Tess' handclasp, such gratitude in her glance, that I felt my own diffidence melting and only a sharp sense of sadness and regret remaining.

I didn't tell a word of Miss Tess' story to anyone but Mom. I could trust her and since she knew of my finding the letter, it seemed only fair to supply the rest of the details and satisfy her natural curiosity. She felt as sorry about it all as I did.

"Still," Mom said, "I can see why she was glad to know the truth. To go through her lifetime, thinking he hadn't really loved her—and then to learn he had—" Mom's voice got chokey.

I nodded. And suddenly the strangeness of the whole situation occurred to me. If I hadn't suggested having a tour of old houses in connection with Centennial Day and if some child whose name I'd never know hadn't eluded me and taken a notion to slide down the banister in the Wentworth house—just thinking about it gave me a queer prickly feeling up and down my spine, as though I were an instrument of fate. . . .

I was very sweet to Brose for a while after that. The memory of Miss Tess' thwarted unhappy love affair somehow seemed to make me appreciate him more than ever. Brose was so solid and dependable and while our relationship wasn't always madly, excitingly romantic, I was very fond of him. And when he kissed me, my heart never failed to lurch as though it were about to turn upside down.

Maybe, I thought, my feeling for him was really love, or something that might well develop into love as we grew a little older. I wondered how a girl could be sure?

Barbie and I got to discussing the question one day when we were having lunch together. "How do you feel," Barbie asked, "when you think about being married to him? That's a good test."

"Wonderful," I said dreamily, stirring my malted around and around with my straw. "I get all queer and soft feeling inside, like gelatine or something."

"I don't," Barbie said flatly, "when I think about marrying Sox. I get kind of perturbed, but not pleasantly so."

I scarcely heard her, so intent was I on my own thoughts. "Brose might be quite wonderful to be married to," I said seriously. "When he's older that is, twenty-three or so. Don't you think that's a good age to get married, Barbie?"

She considered for a moment, chewing her hamburger. Then, "Yes, I guess that's about right. Only honestly, Tobey, I don't imagine Sox will seem like any better husband material to me in five years than he does now. I have a feeling," her voice sank a confidential note lower, "that Sox and I won't do much more than last out the summer."

"What are you saying?" I demanded, my full attention captured at last. "You haven't had a scrap, have you?"

Barbie shook her head. "Maybe it's just that I'm seeing too much of him, working at the same place and all. I mean, it's hard to get palpitations over a man you see every day in a white apron, wrestling canned goods and stuff. The super market just isn't a very glamorous setting, let's face it."

I nodded. I could see her point. "It's entirely different with Brose and me," I admitted. "With both of us working, I haven't seen as much as usual of him this summer. And when I think of his going away out west to school in September, well, it hurts, actually it does. It gives me a sort of lost, empty feeling."

"Ah, September," Barbie positively cooed, her eyes lighting and an enchanting smile curving her mouth. "College. A whole new crop of men to choose from. You mean you're actually going to miss Brose in the midst of all that?"

"I certainly am," I said firmly.

Barbie wagged her head. "Not for long, I'll bet."

I must admit there are times when Barbie isn't very understanding. . . .

By mid-July I had begun to look forward eagerly to our regular yearly vacation at Green Lake. Moving through my routine tasks for Mr. Tweedie, I spent quite a bit of time daydreaming about lazing on the beach, splashing through the clear, chill water, playing tennis and dancing to the juke box at the club. Brose would be there, too, of course. His folks have a cottage right next to ours. It was an entrancing prospect. The only trouble was, it was still a couple of weeks off and the weather was hot and sticky and my job seemed more boring as time wore on.

And then a foul thing developed that made me forget all about my vacation and concentrate on the immediate present, much as I disliked what was happening in it.

Maybe it isn't very nice to refer to Clarissa Hyde as a foul thing, but everyone is entitled to a personal opinion and my opinion of Clarissa was not complimentary. She burst on me so unexpectedly I wasn't at all prepared for her, which may have helped to account for my distaste.

One night when Brose and I were having a bite at Joe's after a movie, he announced out of a clear sky, "A friend of my mother's from California is coming to visit us. A Mrs. Hyde. And she's bringing her daughter with her."

"Oh," I cracked, "any relation to Dr. Jekyll?"

"Very funny," Brose said. "Only if you were having to give up your room so that your parents could sleep in it and let Mrs. Hyde and Clarissa have their room, you wouldn't find it so darn' amusing. Especially since I'm going to have to sleep in the den and the studio couch is lumpy."

"Poor Brose," I patted his hand comfortingly. "My heart bleeds for you. It won't be for long, though, will it?"

"That's it," Brose griped. "We don't know exactly. She and my mother used to be real good friends when they were girls. So they write to each other and we got this letter the other day saying Mrs. Hyde and Clarissa were coming back to Edgewood for a visit and would it be convenient for us to put them up? She didn't say how long and of course my mother couldn't very well ask. She just wrote back and told them we'd *love* to have them. So they're coming Saturday."

"Oh, well," I said philosophically, "it'll probably only be a few days. People from California can never stand the middle west only in very small doses."

"That's what I'm hoping," Brose said with feeling. And then his tone got a little uncomfortable. "There's this complication, though, about Saturday night."

"Oh?"

"Their plane gets in to Chicago around dinner time. So my mother and father are planning to drive in and meet them. And they think I should go along, so we can all have dinner together in town afterward. I told my mother we always have a date on Saturday night, but she said if I explained matters to you she was sure you'd understand."

"And I do, Brose," I said sweetly. "I understand perfectly. As it happens, Dick Allen's going to be home this week end and he wanted me to do something Saturday night with him. So it will work out fine all around, won't it?"

Brose sat there, scowling. But he couldn't very well object under the circumstances. Figuratively, I blew a little kiss at fate for timing things so perfectly. This way I could have a date with Dick, Brose could accommodate his parents and go to meet their guests and there would be no grounds for argument or disappointment on either side.

"Well, don't look so grumpy," I said. "You don't want me to just sit around moping, do you?"

"Fat chance!" Brose growled, finishing off his soda with a loud raucous sound like a Bronx cheer. "What does that navy wolf do, just wait around to pounce till my back's turned?"

"That's not a nice way to talk about Dick," I admonished. "Would you rather I stayed at home while you're having a nice evening out with your friends from California?"

Brose glared at me. "That's not the same thing at all," he said. "It's just something I can't get out of and you know it!"

"Well, all right," I said mildly. "So you can't get out of it. But I'd still be left high and dry on a Saturday night if it didn't just so happen that Dick'll be home."

"Yeah, I guess so," Brose's tone was grudging. "But all the same I don't like it."

"Maybe I don't like your going out with Clarissa, either," I pointed out. "By the way, how old is she?"

"Who cares?" Brose asked morosely. "Fifteen or so, my mother thinks. She isn't quite sure. Anyway, my folks and her mother'll be along—if you call that the same as your having a date with Dick Allen!"

He is really sort of sweet when he gets jealous. "I know," I soothed. "I'm not being very nice, am I?"

There was really no point in letting the situation develop into a quarrel.

I went out with Dick Saturday night and had a wonderful time. We went to a summer theater and saw a revival of *The Desert Song*. The plot seemed rather dated and corny, but the music was so grand, the love scenes so thrilling, I got quite a bang out of it.

Driving home, we hummed tunes from the show and Dick sang *One Alone* in rather a good baritone and with such a warmly personal manner that I was quite stirred.

"I didn't know you had a good voice," I told him.

"There are lots of things about me you don't know," Dick said softly. "We never seem to see each other enough to get very well acquainted."

"Oh, I wouldn't say that," I objected. But it was true in a way. Ever since we'd met last fall, he'd been away at college, or in the navy. Of course, there'd been that football week end at Central and Christmas vacation and the dates we'd had just before he left for Great Lakes. But somehow they hadn't seemed to offer too many chances for self-revealing conversation.

"We could stop right now," Dick said with enthusiasm, "and I could tell you the story of my life."

"Let's not," I said. "I'm vitally interested, but this just doesn't seem like the time and place."

"Afraid I won't limit myself to talking?" Dick asked.

"Maybe a little," I admitted. I said more seriously then, "Dick, our dates really aren't very fair to you."

"Because of Brose?" he asked.

I nodded. "You're such a swell person, you deserve a girl who can give all her thoughts and attention to you, not one with another man on her mind."

"You've got a point there," Dick agreed. "How about forgetting Brose and concentrating on me?"

"That wasn't what I meant," I said.

"I know it," Dick flashed a grin at me, then turned his attention back to the road, "but you might put some serious thought on a switch like that. By the way," he asked then, "where is Brose tonight, or should I just let sleeping dogs lie?"

I told him about the Gilmans' guests from California.

"A break for me," Dick chuckled. "It'd be a bigger break if you two had split up for good, though."

"Nothing like that," I said firmly.

And I didn't kiss him good night, either, although we stood on our front steps discussing the question for almost half an hour. He wasn't easy to resist and there were a couple of times when I almost weakened. But I reminded myself that it wouldn't be fair to encourage him when I really felt he'd do better to find another girl. Nor would it be fair to Brose, stuck as he was with his mother's friends for a dull boring evening.

Had I suspected even faintly what Clarissa was like and what sort of evening Brose was actually having, I wouldn't have struggled with my conscience nearly so hard.

14

Blond bombshell

Our crowd usually gets together somewhere or other on Sunday afternoons and this day being a real scorcher, we decided to head for the pool. Sox and Barbie drove by to pick me up.

"Where's Brose?" Sox asked in surprise as I came down the walk in answer to his honk.

I swung my bathing suit casually from one hand as Barbie opened the door for me. "He hasn't been over today," I admitted. "Of course, they've got company at his house. Maybe he got tied up." I tried to keep my annoyance with Brose's unaccustomed neglect from sounding too obviously through my tone.

"Yeah, that's right," Sox remembered. "He told me some friend of his mother's was coming—and her kid, too. Well, heck, let's swing past there and see if they both wouldn't like to go swimming—Brose and the girl, I mean. Not her mother."

I was secretly pleased with Sox's suggestion. We proceeded to drive to the Gilmans' and Sox swung into the drive and stopped, signaling Brose with the horn in their special way. A minute later Brose came out and loped across the porch and down the steps to join us.

"Hi, Tobey," he said. "Hi, kids. What gives?"

Did I imagine it, or was there something just a little furtive in his manner? It occurred to me he was unusually dressed up, in brown slacks and printed sport shirt and brown and white spectator shoes.

The same idea must have struck Sox, because he said admiringly, "You're looking mighty sharp for such a hot day."

"Oh, well," Brose actually colored a little, "you know how it is when you've got company."

"Yeah," Sox nodded, "I guess so." He asked then, "How about going for a swim? Think this girl who's visiting you would like that?"

"Gee," Brose said, "it sure sounds good. She might like to. I could find out." His glance sought mine and he grinned, sort of hesitantly. "Have fun last night?" he asked.

I nodded. "Did you?"

"It was okay," Brose said. "We had dinner at that new airport restaurant. And then we drove around for a while, showing the Hydes places like Buckingham Fountain and all."

"Sounds peachy swell," Barbie said, "but I'm expiring with the heat. Get the girl and come on before I melt and run away."

"Well, okay," Brose nodded. "I'll see if she wants to."

We waited five minutes, ten, fifteen. The sun beat down on the roof of Sox's car and the wind through the open windows was sickeningly hot. Perspiration ran down our faces. The thought of the pool, mobbed as it would be, seemed like a glorious mirage.

"Honk again, why don't you?" Barbie demanded impatiently.

But Sox admonished, "Keep your hair on. They'll be out in a sec."

It was considerably longer than that before the Gilmans' screen door opened once more and a girl in lime-green shorts, a sleeveless pumpkin-colored shirt and matching thick soled play shoes came out, with Brose close behind her, carrying their swimming suits. She had perfectly straight blond hair, tied high on her neck in one of the most utterly becoming pony tails I had ever seen. She was strikingly beautiful, her tan Indian-copper, her eyes a light greenish-blue beneath lashes as long and dark as any movie star's. And if she was only fifteen, as Brose had intimated, girls must mature very young in California.

As they came toward us, she smiled up at Brose enchantingly and snuggled her hand in his. I swallowed a lump of dismay that was threatening to choke me and tried to pretend I hadn't noticed Barbie's fervent, though whispered, "Wow!" nor the improbable way Sox's eyes had bugged out at sight of Clarissa, like those of some cartoon character.

Murmuring introductions, Brose helped Clarissa into the back seat of the car as if she were something precious and fragile, then climbed in beside her. Of course, he didn't have much choice, since Barbie and Sox and I were all in the front seat. But I felt annoyed with him just the same and far from cordial toward Clarissa. Through a pink mist of rage I glimpsed her fingers still clinging to his, although he didn't seem to be returning her grip with much enthusiasm.

"This is so suh-weet of all of you," Clarissa said in a slow throaty voice. "I just love to swim. At home I spend practically all my time in the water—Daddy swears I must be part mermaid. Do you love to swim, too, Cousin Ambrose?"

Sox sort of choked at that. To call Brose by his real name is not a thing one does lightly. He hates it and has made it so plain to everyone over a period of years, that none of his friends would dream of calling him anything but "Brose." Still, he didn't seem to mind at all what Clarissa called him. There was the silliest, most fatuous look on his face as he smiled at her.

"I didn't know you were cousins," Barbie said.

"Everyone's cousins," Clarissa drawled sweetly, never taking her eyes from Brose's. "Seventh or eighth cousins, I forget which, according to statistics. Of course, there are some people you'd rather be cousins with than others. So the ones I like best, I always call cousin. It makes me feel nice and close to them."

She was certainly sitting close enough to Brose, I thought furiously. The two of them weren't occupying much more than a third of the back seat. Not that I'd have given them the satisfaction of turning around to look. But I could catch a glimpse of them quite clearly in the rear-view mirror.

Brose said, in a slightly strangled tone, "Well, I guess that makes us all cousins, cousins."

And Sox said. "The idea's got possibilities, you know?"

After that, the conversation became more general, but I didn't take much part in it. Barbie squeezed my knee sympathetically.

"Whose pool are we going to swim in?" Clarissa asked.

"It's just the community bathtub," Sox cracked.

And Brose explained to her, "Hardly anybody in Edgewood has a private pool."

"They don't?" Clarissa couldn't have sounded more surprised if she'd heard we still used oil lamps.

"This isn't California, you know," Barbie reminded her. "There are practically no movie stars in town, believe it or not."

"Now you're teasing," Clarissa said reproachfully. "Not everybody in Beverly Hills is in the movies, by any means. But swimming pools—well, they're such a necessity."

"We manage to struggle along, don't we, Ambrose?" Sox said solemnly.

Brose's response was unintelligible. But just then we turned into the long, tree-shaded drive that led to the pool and a muted roar of voices and splashing and squealing met our ears.

Clarissa murmured faintly, "It sounds—crowded."

And Brose told her, "It will be."

"On a hot Sunday like this," Sox added, "you'll do well to find a square foot of water per swimmer. But at least it's wet."

And he wasn't exaggerating—much. Still, the water in the big, blue-lined pool was cool and refreshing, even though you could hardly swim without bumping into someone. We were all used to it, of course, but Clarissa appeared slightly appalled.

Still, she condescended to swim the width of the pool a few times and to do a couple of perfect jackknives off the high platform, her slim rounded body in a stunningly plain white suit flashing through the air like a silver arrow.

"She really is a swell swimmer," I had to admit, albeit grudgingly, to Brose. "But why did you tell me she was only fifteen?"

"My mother was a little off," Brose admitted. "It's kind of hard to keep track of people's age, you know, just in letters. But you don't have to act as if I'm poison, because I was wrong about a little thing like that."

"I'm acting as if you're poison?" I asked loftily. "Don't be silly. Anybody can see this thing between you and Clarissa is bigger than both of you, so why should I get in your way."

Brose gave me a murderous look. "Don't be like that! You know she doesn't mean a thing to me. It's just—well, I can't be unfriendly to her under the circumstances."

I glared at him. "I'd like to hear what you'd say if I held hands with Dick Allen right in front of you!"

"I wasn't," Brose denied. "That is she—well, it's just the way she *is*, Tobey. I mean, she kind of slips her hand into any fella's hand she happens to be with, I imagine, just as a little kid might. Kind of—well, trusting and—like that."

"I don't notice her doing it with Sox," I reminded him.

"That's because she realizes Barbie and he are together."

"And she doesn't realize we are?" I demanded.

"Well, no," Brose admitted. "I don't see how she could. I hadn't got around to telling her about you yet, when you all stopped by. But I will, Tobey, as soon as I have a chance.

"Don't bother," I said icily, "on my account!" And then I saw Clarissa bearing beamingly down on us, so I stalked over to the edge of the pool and jumped in.

By the sheerest good luck, I came up right beside Itchy Stearns. Itchy is sort of good-looking in a dark, lanky way and we have had a few dates at various times without anything at all vital ever coming of it. But right at the moment the sight of any familiar male face was a heartening one for me.

"Itchy!" I smiled at him warmly. "How nice!"

"Fancy meeting you here and stuff like that," Itchy grinned back. Then, "Who's the luscious blond dish with your steady?"

"He's not my steady," I denied through clenched teeth.

"Since when?" Itchy's dark brows climbed inquiringly. "And does Miss America there have anything to do with it?"

"She's just a girl who's visiting his folks," I explained shortly.

"Brother!" Itchy wagged his head. "Nobody like that ever visits us. Our company runs more to skinny ten-year-olds with buck teeth, or old ladies. Is she staying all summer, I hope?"

"How do I know?" I demanded. "If you want to meet her so desperately, why don't you go on up there where you can drool over her at closer range?"

Some note of desperation must have sounded through my tone. Itchy's glance was penetrating for a moment, then he laid a comforting hand on my wet shoulder. "Okay, keed," he murmured, "we'll skip it for now. I guess I can recognize a triangle when I see one. Shall we make it appear to be a four-cornered figure instead? Race you to the deep end."

As we splashed gaily along side by side, I had never felt more kindly toward good old Itchy. And after we had all had enough of swimming, he piled into Sox's car with us, and at least we were an even number, so that I didn't feel as if I were sticking out like a sore thumb while Clarissa lavished all her slightly overwhelming attentions on Brose.

Over sodas at Joe's Grill, I could see Brose growing more and more uncomfortable in the situation in which her attitude put him. But it served him right, I argued with myself, for not telling her last night that I was his girl. Still, I realized in all fairness, it wasn't just the sort of thing he'd announce to her at the moment of their meeting, before she'd even met me. And he hadn't had much chance to tell her anything this afternoon, But I steeled myself against feeling the slightest thrust of sympathy toward him. Anyway, even if Clarissa knew Brose and I were a regular twosome, I doubted it would have made much difference to her. She was just That Kind, I thought. And the fear that she and her mother might be going to make a prolonged stay with the Gilmans haunted me with a special horror.

15

Men are so maddening

The days following the Hydes' arrival in Edgewood were among the longest and most frustrating I have ever lived through. Of course, it wasn't sheer perversity that made Brose sprain his wrist quite badly pruning a tree a few days after they came. But to my annoyed frame of mind, it seemed that way. He had been planning to quit his summer job in another week or so, anyway, so his accident merely made him give it up sooner. But I still had another ten days to work for Mr. Tweedie. So there I was, fretting and fuming away the lovely July days in that hot crowded little office, while Clarissa and Brose were spending practically all their time together. It was almost more than I could take.

I must admit there was no change in Brose's attitude toward me. He had explained to Clarissa that we had been going around together for quite a long while and had every intention of continuing to do so. Clarissa, however, paid little or no attention to this piece of interesting information. She continued to snuggle her hand chummily in Brose's, to gaze up at him with candidly admiring eyes, to smile at him in her childishly provocative manner, whether I was around or not. She tagged along on every date we had, despite my earnest and sometimes not very polite efforts to discourage her. Brose's mother wouldn't let him ditch her, even if he had wanted to, which was definitely a debatable question. Often he was able to line up another boy for Clarissa, but even when we double-dated it was Brose she lavished the greater share of her attention on.

I confided furiously to Barbie, "I'm not even sure he minds the sickening way she hangs after him. He's always making excuses for her and saying she's just a crazy kid and that it's only her way and doesn't really mean anything. But I'm not convinced she's as childlike and candid as she pretends to be."

"Me, either," Barbie agreed. "Although I must admit she's got that act of hers down to perfection. She's about as childlike and candid as a cobra, if you ask me. Only don't expect Brose or any other man to see through her. They're such dopes. Not," Barbie added, "that I'd mind if she went for Sox. I'd just as soon somebody took him off my hands. But Brose is the one she's after, there's no doubt about that."

I gave Barbie a sour look. I didn't need her to tell me that. "One good thing," I gulped miserably, "she won't be around forever."

But the Hydes' visit stretched out, five days, six, a week. Saturday afternoon a crowd of us played tennis on the courts back of the high school. As I should have suspected, Clarissa's game was terrific. We played elimination singles and she trounced one of us after another, male and female. Brose couldn't play on account of his wrist, which was still strapped up, but he cheered her on enthusiastically from the sidelines. I wandered over and sat down on the grass beside him while Clarissa was playing Sox.

"Man, that's some serve!" Brose exclaimed as she sizzled one over so fast poor Sox didn't even come close to it. "She's won several Junior Championships, you know."

"She told me," I said without enthusiasm. "She told everybody." If there's anything I can't stand, it's bragging.

"She doesn't mean to brag," Brose said earnestly, as if he'd read my thoughts. "It's just that she's such a kid, so enthusiastic and outspoken and—"

"Childlike?" I supplied. "Candid?"

"Yeah," Brose nodded, missing my sarcasm entirely.

"I can think of even better adjectives to describe her," I admitted darkly, "only I'm too polite to use them."

Brose frowned unhappily at me. "You just don't understand Clarissa—" he began.

But I cut him off shortly, asking, "Aren't they ever going to leave?"

"Well," Brose said, "I don't know just when. Mrs. Hyde talks about visiting relatives in St. Louis before they go back to the coast, but she hasn't said when she plans to do it. My mother's been kind of wondering, too, because, of course, we'll be going up to Green Lake early in August."

"But that's another week or ten days," I said, appalled.

Brose nodded. But I didn't notice him complaining about having to give up his room any more, or to sleep on a lumpy studio couch. All he said was, "Maybe they won't stay that long."

I twisted a blade of grass on the ground between us. Brose laid his hand over mine, but I pulled away out of sheer contrariness.

"What's wrong with you lately?" Brose scowled.

I glared right back at him. "Maybe I don't like having

my hand held by someone who's always holding hands with someone else!"

A slow grin curved Brose's mouth. "You wouldn't be jealous of a crazy kid like Clarissa?"

"Certainly not!" I said positively. "She simply does not appeal to me, that's all. And ever since she's been here I haven't been able to get her out of my hair!"

Brose chuckled. "You're real cute when you're jealous."

If I hadn't left my racquet lying some distance off, I'd have bopped him with it. I was that mad!

I guess Brose could tell I was, too. Because he said soothingly, "Okay, okay, I won't tease you any more." Then, in a changing-the-subject sort of tone, he asked, "What'll we do tonight?"

"Are we going to do anything?" I asked loftily.

"Don't be like that," Brose coaxed. "You know we always have a date on Saturday nights. There's a swell movie at the drive-in."

I had already checked on that. "Will we have to take you-know-who?" I demanded.

Brose looked apologetic. "I guess so. I've been trying to line up another guy for her, but Saturday night's a rough time to find anybody loose. Do you mind a lot?"

"It'll simply *make* my evening," I snapped.

Of course, I could have refused to go, but why should I give Clarissa the satisfaction of having Brose all to herself?

She and Sox strolled up just then, laughing and talking. Her pale hair shone like gilt in the sunshine and her white shorts and halter were scarcely wrinkled for all her exertion. She had beaten Sox soundly, but he didn't seem to care. Seeing the kind of dreamy way he smiled down at Clarissa, I had a hunch that Barbie might have been able to get rid of him without much trouble, if Clarissa had offered him even a little encouragement. But her maddeningly lovely face lit up like a whole string of Japanese lanterns as she beamed at Brose. And she said, "I'll bet you could beat me, Cousin Ambrose, if you were able to play."

"I doubt it," Brose admitted with unaccustomed modesty. "That serve of yours is murder."

She'd probably lose on purpose, I thought acidly, if she were playing with Brose. I wouldn't put even that corny trick past her. . . .

Just as I was climbing out of the shower an hour or so later, I heard the phone ring. Midge answered it and sang out, "It's for you, Tobey. You out of the tub?"

Honestly, little sisters! A girl certainly has no secrets with them around. I draped a bath towel around me, sarong fashion, and padded out to take the phone from Midge, giving her a dirty look.

"I think it's Dick," she said.

This I doubted, but sure enough, Midge was right. I managed to shoo her away, although her intention was obviously to hang around and listen. When I had got rid of her, I asked Dick, "What in the world are you doing home? You had a pass last week end."

"Who knows?" Dick chuckled. "The ways of the navy are past all understanding. Probably I won't get another one for a month, so let's make this one memorable, shall we?"

"Oh, Dick, I can't—" I began. And then I stopped, an idea occurring to me. "Unless, that is," I amended, "you'd care to go on a double date with Brose and a girl named Clarissa Hyde who's visiting him and his folks."

"You mean," Dick asked, his voice a little puzzled, "this Clarissa and I would go with you and Brose?"

"Well, sort of," I explained, with a little giggle. "Only

whoever Clarissa goes with, it's Brose she really concentrates on, so—" I left it at that.

"So," Dick picked it up, "that would leave me free to devote most of my attention to you?"

"Something like that," I admitted. I went on then to explain about Clarissa's annoying ways in a bit more detail.

When I had finished, Dick said, "Well, it isn't exactly the sort of evening I had in mind, but if it means seeing you, I won't quibble. What time shall I come over?"

We settled that and talked for a few minutes longer. As soon as Dick had hung up, I called Brose.

"Guess what," I said brightly. "I've got a date for Clarissa tonight, so we can double after all."

"Who?" Brose asked interestedly. "I thought I'd tried everybody."

"Dick Allen," I told him. "He's in town again."

There was a small silence at the other end of the wire. Finally Brose said, "Oh?" in a noncommittal sort of tone.

"Of course," I said sweetly, "if you'd rather not double with Dick, I suppose I could go out with him and you could take Clarissa to the drive-in, since you're going to have to take her anyway."

"Nothing doing," Brose said flatly. "The four of us will go. It's just—well, he's pretty old for her and I can't imagine they'll be very congenial, but—I guess it's okay. . . ."

Dick had his folks' car that night and the Gilmans wanted to use theirs, so Dick drove by and picked me up first. Then we stopped by for Clarissa and Brose.

I guess maybe I should have told Dick she was sort of spectacular looking, prepared him just a little. When she came down the Gilmans' front walk with Brose, I couldn't help noticing the way Dick's eyes opened wide. He sort of straightened up in the seat beside me and smoothed his collar down and tugged at his tie. Clarissa was wearing a turquoise-colored dress that matched her eyes and left a lot of her tanned throat and shoulders bare. She must have been wearing platform soles, too, because she looked taller, more mature somehow. Her hair was tied high on her neck with a black velvet ribbon.

As Brose murmured introductions, her black-lashed eyes were fixed unwaveringly on Dick's face and an enchanting little smile curled her mouth. And Dick simply stared at her, almost unbelievingly, the silliest, most fatuous smile distorting his usually handsome and intelligent-looking features.

Still looking at Dick, Clarissa addressed me in her slow, beguiling drawl. "Well, Tobey," she asked, "aren't you going to get into the back seat with Cousin Ambrose?"

I gulped something unintelligible. Any other time, Clarissa would have hung onto Brose's hand so hard he couldn't get away from her. But not tonight, not with Dick around. Clarissa had a sort of dazzled gleam in her eye, such as some girls get at the mere sight of a man in uniform.

"Come on, Tobey." Brose held the door for me and there was nothing I could do but slide out and get into the back seat with him as Clarissa settled her full skirts daintily beside Dick.

Somehow things weren't working out at all as I had planned them. Of course, my date had been with Brose all along. But I'd figured Clarissa would cling to him as she usually did, which would throw Dick and me together, while Brose simply writhed internally to see us. And now here was Clarissa, taking Dick over just as she had taken Brose at the start. Honestly, I had never known such an annoying unpredictable person, never in my whole life!

I overheard Dick say to Clarissa, "I didn't know you and Brose were cousins."

And Clarissa answered, with her clear, childlike little laugh, "Well, everybody's cousins according to statistics. Eighth, I think it is. And I sort of like to call my very favorite people 'cousin.' It makes them seem closer somehow, Cousin Dick."

I stopped listening then and turned my full attention to Brose, who was saying something to me in a very low, confidential tone, almost a whisper. But all I caught was the one word, "Tuesday," so I had to ask him to repeat it.

He leaned over and with his lips so close against my ear that his breath sort of tickled, said, "They're leaving next Tuesday. Her mother said so at dinner."

I looked at him penetratingly to see if he seemed sorry. But there was a cheerful grin on his face as he looked back at me. Even the sight of Clarissa, pressing her shoulder hard against Dick's in the front seat didn't seem to bother him in the slightest. In fact, I discovered somewhat to my surprise, it didn't actually bother me, either. Let her concentrate on Dick if she wanted to. Let Dick act perfectly silly about her. The sight of the two of them, practically drooling over each other wasn't nearly so painful as it had been when she was using all her wiles on Brose.

Suddenly, I realized that I was feeling very happy. In elaborate pantomime I pointed first at Clarissa, then at Dick, then held up two fingers very close together to indicate how well they seemed to be getting along.

Brose nodded, grinning.

"Don't you mind?" I murmured.

"Mind?" Brose whispered back, his eyebrows rising in genuine surprise. "Why should I? All I was worried about was that he'd think he was taking you out and I'd be stuck with her."

He put his arm along the back of the seat behind me and I snuggled against him, relief rising in me like a warm tide. Even if Dick wouldn't be here to occupy Clarissa's attention except for this one evening, I could easily stick it out till next Tuesday. Three days? Why, they'd fly past before I knew it. Particularly with Brose not caring what she did, not caring a single teensy bit.

16

Green Lake

As I HAD EXPECTED, TUESDAY CAME and Clarissa departed almost before I knew it. I was so busy that last week at the office, winding up a lot of stuff for Mr. Tweedie and trying to get ready to leave on my vacation, that I didn't have much time to think about Clarissa. When I did have a minute for remembering, I had to admit that the tizzy I had let myself get into over her seemed a little silly. Not that I'd have acknowledged it out loud. Especially not to Brose.

I could just imagine his insufferably tolerant smile and the way he'd say, "I told you all along she was just a crazy kid. The way she fell for Dick's uniform proves it."

No, I wouldn't give him the satisfaction. And apparently Brose felt, too, that the whole Clarissa incident would be better ignored and forgotten. Because he didn't say anything about her, either, after she'd gone. And each of us was especially nice to the other, which made our dates more enjoyable than ever.

We were both looking forward to the weeks we'd spend at the lake. The Gilmans always tried to go up at the same time we did. Brose's father and mine liked to fish together, our mothers were quite good friends and, of course, neither Brose nor I could imagine Green Lake without the other.

In a way, we were anticipating our vacation more than ever this year. Before long we'd be separated, Brose at one college and I at another, hundreds of miles apart. Every time I thought of it, a queer lost feeling settled over me. Did Brose feel the same, I wondered?

He brought up the subject himself on our last date before leaving Edgewood. We were taking a little drive after a party at Barbie's house. The night was lovely, moonlit and starspangled. Rain that afternoon had left everything smelling fresh and clean.

We were just driving along, not saying much, when out of a clear sky, Brose exclaimed, "Gosh, Tobey, when I think of going clear out to Colorado to school, not seeing you for months on end, it's rough!"

"I know," I admitted, my throat aching.

"Like I was losing my right arm, or something," Brose went on. "How am I going to get along without you?"

"You'll manage." I tried to sound sensible and mature, but my voice cracked a little. "We'll both manage. We'll have to."

Things like this happened to people all the time, I reminded myself. Hundreds of couples, thousands, who had gone around together during high school, who had come to depend on each other for fun and companionship. Maybe the feeling between them was no stronger than friendship, maybe it had in it the roots of a much deeper attachment. Either way, it hurt breaking it off. It hurt a lot.

"I'll never feel this way about another girl," Brose's

voice was husky.

"You think so now," I gulped, "but when you're away—" I couldn't seem to force any more words past the lump in my throat.

Brose braked the car at the side of the road. He reached out and gathered me close into his arms and it was a wonderful place to be, warm and safe, the future shut away, only the present important. Our lips met and feeling surged up in me, making my pulses pound.

After a minute I pulled away and said, with a shaky attempt at laughter, "I guess that proves your point."

Brose's arm stayed around me. "Sometimes," he said unhappily, "I wish I hadn't planned to go to college."

"Don't be silly," I told him. "You know you want to, really. And your folks want you to go. It's all settled. We can't upset everybody's plans just because we'll miss each other."

"I could have gone to Central, where you'll be," Brose argued. "Only Colorado was my dad's school and he had such a yen for me to go there, too."

"Maybe it'll be a good thing for us to be apart," I admitted. "Dating other people, we'll have a chance to find out if we really mean as much to each other as we think now."

"Maybe so," Brose said grudgingly, "but I don't like the idea. You're my girl, Tobey. We understand each other so well, we've had so much fun together."

I nodded. But then I said, "Don't sound as if we're going our separate ways tomorrow. We'll have weeks at the lake of seeing each other every day. Why, you'll probably get so tired of me, you'll be glad to go to college."

"Fat chance," Brose denied morosely.

Some demon of mischief prompted me to remind him,

"Or maybe I won't see so much of you at Green Lake. Remember last year? Remember Kentucky Jackson?"

Brose frowned. "What a time to bring her up. I can't even remember how she looked."

"I can," I teased. "And I remember that deep-South drawl of hers and the perfectly mad pash you had for her. Who knows, maybe there'll be somebody this year who'll turn your head."

Brose started the motor with an angry jerk. Honestly, I don't know why I get such a bang out of tormenting the guy when I really like him so well. . . .

We drove up to Green Lake the following Saturday. Mom and Dad sat in the front seat, Midge and I in the back. We had enough luggage loaded in the trunk and on the floor to stock a safari heading into the jungle. All of us were in high spirits. There seems to be a sort of special mood that comes over people who are leaving home on a vacation trip, a kind of care-free-ness, a sense of escape from familiar routine and problems. Life at the lake was always easy and informal, aside from the initial job of getting the cottage into shape after it had been closed up so long. And this year, we were even going to avoid that chore. Alicia and Adam had been using it for two weeks and they'd have the place pretty well in condition. They planned to leave the day after we arrived, as the cottage wasn't big enough to hold us all comfortably. Besides, they had things to do at home, getting ready for Adam to go back to college, lining up living quarters at Central for the two of them and all.

It's only a few hours' drive from Edgewood to Green Lake. Alicia had a nice luncheon ready when we arrived, the table laid on the screened porch where it was shady and cool. She and Adam looked wonderfully relaxed and rested. Alicia, who is somewhat the hothouse type, never goes in for tanning. But Adam was Indian-brown.

We lingered over dessert and iced tea, talking and laughing. We told Alicia and Adam all the things that had happened in Edgewood since they left. And they briefed us on who was at the lake and who had already gone home, how the fishing and swimming were and so on. This would be the first year I'd been at the lake when Barbie Walters wasn't. She and her family had gone to visit relatives in Connecticut instead of opening up their lake cottage. But Alicia assured me that several friends of mine were around, Kay Lamb and Itchy Stearns and some others.

"Oh, and the most exciting thing!" Alicia told us, her eyes sort of lighting up. "We have an Art Colony at the lake this year. Can you imagine?"

Frankly, I couldn't. The summer crowd at Green Lake had never shown the slightest leaning toward art, so far as I could remember. Swimming and fishing and boating had been their main interests.

"An Art Colony?" my father repeated incredulously. "What's the place coming to? Aren't the fish biting this summer?"

"Sure, they are," Adam said, scowling. "And the swimming's fine, too. But that's not enough for some people."

I was quite intrigued, myself. I asked Alicia, "What do you mean by an Art Colony exactly?"

Before she could answer, Adam put in, "A bunch of dopey females who imagine they can paint, egged on and encouraged by as screwy a character as you ever saw, one Christopher Claypool."

I hadn't often heard my brother-in-law sound so bitter.

And to my astonishment, Alicia glared at him furiously, denying, "He's nothing of the sort, and you know it! He's a fine artist and a very wonderful person. Just because you have simply no conception of what modern art means—"

Adam didn't even wait for her to finish. He broke in, "If understanding modern art means admiring paintings that look as though a moronic four-year-old ran wild with the contents of his paintbox, then I guess I don't." He appealed to my father, man to man, "Honestly, what do you think of this surrealist lunacy?"

My father asked, "You mean stuff like that painting of the limp watch, bent halfway over the edge of a table?"

"That's Dali," Alicia said. "Chris doesn't go along with Dali's ideas at all."

"Dali's pictures make more sense than Claypool's," Adam insisted. "And when you see some of the efforts of his band of faithful followers, you'll really feel sick."

Alicia said icily, "Chris is a wonderful artist! And he feels that art is an experience in which everyone should participate. It enlarges one's viewpoint, sets one free."

"Now you're quoting that crackpot," Adam accused. "The man's a poseur and a complete exhibitionist, if you ask me."

"Nobody did!" Alicia snapped. And, pushing her chair back, she got to her feet and proceeded to start stacking the dishes so recklessly I feared for them.

I hadn't heard her and Adam argue like this since before they were married. They used to have disagreements that were dillies then. In fact, some of their quarrels were so violent, it had been doubtful for a time if they'd ever get as far as the altar. But since their marriage, they'd got along like a pair of cooing doves, so far as I could tell.

What sort of person was this Christopher Claypool, I wondered, that he could spark such a storm of controversy between them?

All of us proceeded to pour oil on the troubled waters like mad and change the subject as fast as possible. But curiosity about the Art Colony and the man responsible for it continued to gnaw at me. As soon as the dishes were out of the way, I announced my intention of going down to the beach. Midge was already off swimming with some of her cronies. Mom and Dad decided that the breeze seemed a bit cool and that they'd wait till a little later. And Adam, obviously trying to worm his way back into Alicia's good graces, persuaded her to go canoeing with him. So I put on my new white bathing suit and started along the path toward the beach alone.

There was really no use stopping by for Brose, since I knew he'd be helping clean up the Gilmans' cottage. But since the path passed their door, I did peer in through the screen and call, "Yoo-hoo, Brose. Going swimming?"

He came out onto the porch in an old disreputable pair of dungarees and a dirty tee-shirt, his hair grayed with cobwebs and a dripping scrubbing brush in one hand.

"The luck of some people!" he griped. "I'll be tied up for hours yet. Can't you wait?"

I shook my head. "Come down when you're through," I suggested. "I'll probably still be there. I want to absorb lots of sunshine and see Kay and the gang. I'm sorry you can't come now, too."

His mother called him then, so I waved good-bye and walked on down toward the beach. The dust of the path was warm and squishy between my bare toes, the special smell of the lake came to meet me like an old familiar friend.

It looked just the same as always as I glimpsed it through the trees, blue-green and tranquil, the yellow crescent of the sandy beach lapped by the water, the dark green blob of Gull Island a little way offshore standing out in sharp relief. Midge and some of her pals were splashing around and yelling at each other just a little way out. There were a few sun-baskers on the diving float, swimmers' heads bobbed here and there, although the beach wouldn't get really crowded until a little later in the day. And then I saw something that offered the final convincing proof that things were a bit different this summer at Green Lake after all.

My eyes widening in astonishment, although, goodness knows, I'd been warned by that scene at luncheon, I noticed that there were three easels set up on the beach. And at each of them a feminine artist worked diligently. Two of them were strangers to me, but the third, I realized with a start as I drew nearer, was Kay Lamb.

I had known Kay since we were in grade school and I couldn't recall ever having seen her with a paintbrush in her hand before. Yet there she sat on the sand before her easel, painting away as though her life depended on it. She was wearing a bathing suit and a wide-beaked denim cap and one of her most earnest expressions, eyes squinted, lips pursed, a wrinkle of concentration between her brows.

If Kay had fallen under the spell of Christopher Claypool, she should be able to tell me all about him, I realized, as I ran the last few steps toward her, unable to wait longer for more details.

17

All about Chris

"DARLING!" KAY'S FACE BRIGHTENED AS she glanced up to see me bearing down on her. "How wonderful you've arrived!"

She gave me a friendly little hug and we talked for a few minutes about who was at the lake and what had been happening and so on. Then Kay turned solemnly back to her painting. I moved around behind her and took a look for myself.

"What is it?" I gasped, when I could speak.

Kay said gently, "Darling, one doesn't ask 'what is it?' about modern art. It's whatever it makes you feel inside."

The only way Kay's meaningless dabs and scrabbles of blue paint, highlighted with greenish yellow, made me feel was slightly sick, although, of course, I was too tactful to say so.

"It must be the lake," I groped apologetically. I felt fairly safe in guessing that, with all the blue on her canvas.

Kay nodded. "Of course, it is. And this yellow is sunshine." She indicated several bright flecks that looked more as though someone had bit into a hot dog too enthusiastically and sprinkled the picture with mustard.

I shook my head. "I guess a person has to know more about it than I do, in order to understand this sort of art."

Kay said, with a faint sigh and a definitely dreamy look in her dark eyes, "Wait till you meet Chris, pet. He's simply wonderful. And so lucid! He makes everything quite clear."

"Alicia spoke of him, too," I told Kay. "I'm dying to hear more. But I couldn't ask her a lot of questions, because Adam just went into a tailspin when she mentioned him."

Kay smiled ironically. "Itchy Stearns reacts in exactly the same way. Practically all the men around do. It's because Chris is so perfectly fascinating he has all the girls hanging on his slightest word, so naturally the men dislike him. He's very masculine, though, not at all the sissy artist type. Honestly, it simply stirs you up to think of him."

"But where did he come from?" I demanded, growing more intrigued by the minute. "What's he doing here? Tell me!"

Kay proceeded to do so. It seemed that Chris Claypool was from Chicago. He was a nephew of the Fletchers who, years and years before, had built a great ornate summer home overlooking the lake, complete with private pier and boathouse. Everyone referred to it jokingly as Fletchers' Folly, although the sign on the massive stone gatepost read HAWK'S REST—J. P. FLETCHER. No one had occupied the house for as long as I could remember, although there was some sort of arrangement with a local resident to take care of it, so that it had never fallen into disrepair. And now, it seemed, Chris Claypool had inherited it. His first intention had been to sell it at once. But he had liked the old place so well at first sight, according to Kay, that he had decided to take a two months' leave of absence from his job as a commercial artist and spend the summer at Green Lake.

"Commercial art," Kay explained, adding a dash of bright red to her already vivid painting, "stifles Chris. He's always simply yearned to let himself go and paint as he wants to. So now he's doing just that. And he's so enthusiastic and forceful, he's got a whole lot of other people interested in expressing themselves, too. Oh, Tobey, you just can't help catching fire from him. He's a complete individualist. Every other man you've known seems utterly tame and inane and colorless by comparison."

"How old is he?" I managed to put in.

Kay shrugged. "Chris is timeless. You just don't think of age in connection with him, either his or your own. He makes you feel like a feather, floating on the wind, airy and free."

I had a hunch Kay was quoting the fabulous Chris. She certainly didn't sound like herself. In response to my increasingly questioning look, she finally said, "Oh, I suppose he's in his late twenties, or very early thirties. But sometimes you'd think he was sixteen and sometimes sixty, depending on his mood. He's the most vital, the most fascinating, the most completely original personality I've ever known. You'll feel that way, too."

Certainly he didn't sound dull, I thought. But I had no intention of spending the rest of the day talking about him.

"Since he isn't around," I suggested, buckling on my bathing cap, "how about a swim?"

"Oh, not right now," Kay's tone was reproving. "I want to finish my picture first, before the light changes."

How she could tell whether it was finished or not, I

couldn't exactly see, but naturally I didn't say so.

I went splashing out into the water and it was as grand as it looked, cool and invigorating. I swam to the raft and climbed the ladder. The girls I had seen sunning themselves proved to be much younger than I. No one else around except a couple of boys about the same age as the girls. They kept diving in all sorts of crazy ways to attract the girls' attention and kept the whole raft jiggling with their antics. I lay down on my tummy and buried my face in my crossed arms. These kids made me feel quite old and mature and I wasn't entirely sure I liked the sensation. The girls kept giggling at the boys' humorous remarks, which spurred them on to even greater efforts to be witty.

Had I actually been that young, I wondered, only a few years ago? It just didn't seem possible! I found myself wishing that Brose would come down to the beach and swim out to join me. Or that Kay would finish her silly painting. Or even that Itchy or anyone else I knew, for that matter, would turn up. I felt lonesome and left out of things, a little sorry for myself.

Finally I got tired of being stepped over and sprinkled with water every time one of the boys dived and then clambered back up onto the raft. I got up and dived into the water myself. My crawl was pretty smooth and there seemed to be a sort of restless urge in me that could only be satisfied by action. I swam on and on, parallel with the shore, never so far out as to be in danger in case I tired, enjoying the coolness of the water and the contrasting heat of the sunshine.

Somewhere up this way, I remembered, there was a tiny stretch of beach where Brose and I sometimes used to swim and lie for a while on the white sand, liking the sense of complete privacy it gave us, the illusion of being shut off from the world. I lifted my head, treading water for a few seconds, and looked around to get my bearings. The little beach was just ahead of me, so I swam in until I could feel solid ground beneath my feet, then walked up to the sunny, rock-surrounded triangle of sand.

It was deserted as usual and so quiet it seemed hard to realize how close it actually was to the big main beach. The voices from there were muted, only the little waves lapping at the shore and the whisper of breeze in the surrounding foliage made any discernible sound. I was more tired than I had thought. I dropped down onto the sand, threw an arm across my eyes to shade them, and lay there, breathing rather deeply for a few minutes. Certainly I hadn't figured on falling asleep, but that was exactly what I did.

When I awoke, my first impression was of confusion. I couldn't remember where I was, or what I was doing there. I sat up hastily, feeling hot and sandy.

"Don't do that," a masculine voice said firmly. "I'm painting you."

I turned my head in astonishment and looked up at a strange young man in Tahitian-patterned swimming trunks. He had very black hair, close-cut and rather bristly, bright blue eyes and a nice smile. He was surveying me thoughtfully over the top of an artist's easel, on which he proceeded to dab paint with the same sort of enthusiastic concentration I had noted in Kay awhile ago.

"Don't tell me you're a disciple of Claypool's, too," I said. "I thought they were all female."

He chuckled. "I guess most of them are. Why?" he asked then, fixing me with his electric glance. "Don't you like art?"

"Oh, definitely," I said, "in its place. But summer vacation at a lake—well, what's wrong with swimming and boating and that sort of thing?"

"Art," the young man said after a thoughtful moment during which his rather oddly disturbing gaze never left my face, "has no place, as you put it. Art is too large, too all-embracing, too universal to be shoved into any neat little cubbyhole and labeled, 'For use only at such and such a time and under such and such circumstances.' Swimming and boating are fine and I'm for them. In fact, I may decide to go swimming any minute. See, I'm all prepared." He touched his gaudy trunks with the end of his paint brush. "But when I come to the beach, I always bring my paints along, too, just in case I happen on any sleeping nymphs, as I was lucky enough to do today. And now, if you wouldn't mind resuming the position you were in, flat on your back, one knee up and your arm thrown across your eyes, I can get on with my painting."

No slightest doubt remained in my mind by the time he was finished with that speech. "You're Christopher Claypool, aren't you?" I asked in rather a small voice, meekly lying down again as I'd been told. And then, struck by sudden realization, "And this is your private beach. No one's lived here for so long I'd forgotten. I'm terribly sorry."

"That's all right. I like company." He flashed his beguiling grin at me. "Who are you?" he asked.

I told him and we proceeded to talk easily while he painted. I explained that I was Alicia Wentworth's sister and Chris Claypool said, "Ah, Alicia, the lily maid of Astolat, or, to be more accurate, of Green Lake. Hers is a face such as sent armored knights to high adventure. She belongs in another time and place, along with Guinevere, Elaine, the ivied towers of Old England, the Round Table—" he broke off then to stare at me fixedly. "You don't look a bit like her," he said.

"Well, thanks," I murmured coldly, starting to sit up.

But he said vehemently, "Stay put, will you, till I'm finished? I didn't mean to imply you aren't beautiful, too. You are, but in a warmer, gayer, more contemporary manner. Alicia is aloof, while you—you're—" he hesitated.

"Be sure it's flattering now," I laughed, "or I may not pose any longer."

He laughed, too, giving his canvas a quick decisive tap with his brush, as though he were dotting an "i". "There, it's finished. So anything I say about you now has no ulterior motivation whatever. Your face is the sort that draws people close, as though to warm themselves. There's fire in you and—" he broke off, staring out toward the water. "Would this irate young man striding toward us be looking for you? I have never laid eyes on him before, so it can't be me he's after."

I sat up quickly and sure enough, it was Brose wading up out of the water.

"For Pete's sake, Tobey," he growled, "what's the idea scaring me like that? Kay said you swam out to the raft and the kids out there said you headed up this way. I was about ready to start sounding an alarm when I remembered this little beach and thought I'd check on whether you came here."

"I'm sorry," I apologized. "I didn't mean to scare you. I was just swimming around and I thought of this place, so I swam in. Then I fell asleep and Mr. Claypool started painting me—" I realized belatedly that they hadn't met. In response to my introduction, they shook hands, although Brose still looked grumpy.

"Painting you?" he repeated dubiously.

"Mr. Claypool is an artist," I explained. "He's aroused a lot of interest in art here at Green Lake. Didn't you see Kay's painting?"

"That was a painting?" Brose laughed. "Thanks for telling me."

A rather pained look settled on Chris Claypool's face. "I take it," he said, "you don't think much of modern art?"

"Well, in a word, no," Brose admitted. "It's screwball, if you ask me. I think a picture ought to look like the thing it's a picture of. You see what I mean?"

"Oh, perfectly," Chris Claypool said. "That's all been taken care of, though, by the invention of the camera. In painting, it isn't so much what the eye records that's important, but the impact made on one's brain, one's imagination."

"You—paint that way, too?" Brose sort of gulped.

"Take a look for yourself," Chris suggested.

I followed Brose over to stand beside Chris and stare at his painting. It was a lot of blue squiggles with a kind of beige blob off to one side. There was a smaller coppery blob near the beige one. My hair, I wondered? And was the shapeless beige blob me? If this was the way I made Chris Claypool feel, should I be flattered, or indignant?

"It leaves you speechless, doesn't it?" Chris's tone was low and warmly personal, for me alone, I felt.

"I—don't understand it," I admitted hesitantly.

"Who could?" Brose asked rather loudly. He glared belligerently at Chris. "I think it's a low trick to tell a girl you're painting her picture and then make a mish-mash like this!"

Chris's bright blue glance met mine in a quick, secret

look that shut Brose out as effectively as a six-foot fence. "You don't feel that way, too?" His tone implied that only my opinion was important.

"No," I said firmly, moved by an absolutely irresistible urge to take Chris's side in the argument. "No, I don't. Brose just doesn't know much about art, that's all. I don't, either, really. But I'd like to learn."

Brose looked at me as though I'd stabbed him in the back.

But I didn't care, with Chris's smile warming me. He was wonderful, I thought, just as Kay and Alicia had said. And maybe, if I got some paints and stuff for myself, he'd teach me something about this intriguing new art form, just as he had them. What a completely different and enthralling way to spend a vacation, I reflected, with a little fluttering sort of sigh.

18

Feminine strategy

ALICIA AND ADAM LEFT FOR HOME ON Sunday afternoon. Adam had some caustic remarks to make about Alicia's paintings taking up so much room in the trunk of their convertible that there was hardly any space left for their luggage.

"You just see to it," Alicia warned, "that you haven't packed things so my paintings will be ruined."

"Why, baby," Adam said with a sardonic grin, "you know I wouldn't do that. Just think of the tone they'll lend to our quonset, or two-room apartment, or whatever we turn out to be living in at college. We'll be the envy of the campus."

Alicia has practically no sense of humor. And she never could stand sarcasm. She glared at Adam and accused, "You're simply jealous because you have no artistic talent whatever!"

"I know I don't," Adam glared right back. "That makes me different than some I could mention!"

Alicia said icily. "Chris says my work shows great imagination. He says I have a feeling for color that is quite rare in a beginner. I think I'll take some art courses in college."

"That makes sense," Adam agreed. "But they won't teach you this crazy modern stuff there."

Alicia ignored him. "I wonder," she reflected, "whether formal art training would spoil my originality?"

Adam opened his mouth to speak, then seemed to think better of it. I guess a year of marriage had taught him just how far it was safe to go with Alicia.

"I don't think it would," I said, to bridge the lengthening silence. I went on to tell them about Chris Claypool having painted a picture of me the previous afternoon.

"I'll bet your best friend wouldn't recognize you in it." Adam stowed away the last suitcase and slammed the trunk lid down.

"Well, no, I guess not," I admitted. "But it was exciting, anyway, to have him use me as a model. You know, I think I'll have to try painting a little. Everyone else seems to be getting such a bang out of it."

"Et tu, Tobey?" Adam wagged his head reproachfully.

"Oh, you'll love it," Alicia told me enthusiastically. "Would you like to borrow my paints? I'll probably be too busy to use them much, anyway, before you get back home."

"That would be wonderful," I said, "if you don't mind."

Alicia proceeded to make Adam open up the car trunk again, so she could get the paints for me. But he didn't seem to care a bit. In fact, the unobtrusive wink he gave me behind her back indicated that he thought I was just pretending to want to use them in order to discourage Alicia's further efforts along artistic lines. And since I had no chance to set him straight on the matter, he pressed my hand with real affection in good-bye and whispered, "I'll do you a good turn someday, too, kid."

Mom and Dad and Midge and I all stood waving to them as they drove off. Then Dad said, "Well, guess I'll take the boat out and see if the fish are biting. Want to come along, any of you?" His invitation sounded polite, rather than enthusiastic.

But Midge was going swimming and Mom had promised Mrs. Gilman she'd drop over. I knew darned well Dad didn't want me along. I jiggled the boat too much, he always said. And I guess I did. It seems such a terrific waste of time to me, spending hours just sitting and waiting for a fish to bite. And none of us like fish too well, anyway. Besides, they're such a nasty job to clean.

"Okay," Dad said and started off cheerfully, his new casting rod over his shoulder.

"Isn't it funny," Mom said fondly, her glance following him, "how many different things a vacation at the lake means to different people? Dad likes fishing, you girls swim most of the time and I just like being lazy and relaxing and getting out of my familiar routine."

I nodded. "Only this year something new has been added. Art." That was all I said aloud. But to myself I breathed meaningfully, "*And* Chris Claypool."

"Art," Mom smiled and shook her head. "It doesn't exactly fit in with the usual lake activities. But Alicia was certainly enthusiastic about it. She gets poor Adam so mad."

"Not just Alicia," I told Mom. "Kay Lamb was painting down on the beach yesterday instead of swimming. Almost everywhere you look there's an amateur artist working away."

"Some of the stuff they paint is crazy," Midge stated flatly. "I looked over some of their shoulders, and yipes!"

"In modern art," I tried to explain to my little sister, "you don't paint things as they look. You paint the way they make you feel inside. I don't know much about it, but I know that much. And I'd like to learn more."

Midge sniffed. "I'd rather swim any day." She trotted off toward the back yard, where her bathing suit hung on the line.

"Bring mine, too, will you?" I called after her.

It was quite a hot day and I knew Brose would want to swim. And, after all, I couldn't very well start painting till I'd learned a little more about it. . . .

Brose and I walked down to the beach hand in hand, along the path we had traveled so often in the past. The sun came dappling down through the trees and a little breeze ruffled my hair forward into my eyes.

"Sheep dog," Brose teased, and pulled me close for just a minute under a big oak tree. Our lips met and my heart made a queer lurching movement. Then we walked on toward the lake, our hands clasped a little tighter.

"Darn it," Brose said, "I wish we were going to be here longer than just three measly weeks."

"It's more than that," I reminded, "counting week ends."

"Still too short," Brose argued. "Unless," he added, "that Claypool character is going to give me trouble."

"He's far too busy to waste time on me," I said, hoping not a word of it was true.

"I don't know," Brose objected. "He seemed perfectly willing to waste time painting your picture." He laughed then, a rather unpleasnt snort of merriment. "What a picture! It looked like a mess of spaghetti or something on a cracked blue plate."

"Honestly!" I exclaimed. "The ignorance of some people!"

But we had reached the beach by that time and a crowd of our friends surrounded us, so we had no opportunity to continue the discussion. Which was probably just as well. Kay and Itchy were in swimming today, along with several others we knew well from previous summers. We splashed into the water and swam out to the raft. We dived and ducked each other and lay in the bright sunshine, talking and laughing and tossing good-humored insults at everyone in sight. It was just as other summers at Green Lake had been. In fact, I realized, there wasn't an amateur artist around.

Brose remarked about this, adding sarcastically, "Maybe the art union makes them take Sundays off. How about it, Kay?"

"Very funny," Kay said.

Itchy sneered, "Now, Brose, we don't make light of Art that way. Wait till you go to one of Claypool's classy saloons and get educated."

"The word is *salon* and you know it," Kay corrected coldly. "You're just trying to be obnoxious."

"I'm succeeding, too," Itchy agreed cheerfully. "But the fact remains, he holds these fancy doings every Sunday night and all us yokels are invited. Only reason I go," Itchy admitted, "is because Kay loves to and the food's fair."

Kay gave him a nasty look.

But before they could get into a good fight, I asked, "Does he really have some sort of get-together every Sunday night? And is everyone really invited?"

Kay nodded. "They're just wonderful, Tobey. You'll love them. They're sort of like Open Houses, with everyone coming and going and it's so fascinating. Lots of Chris's pictures are on display and, of course, the Fletcher house is perfectly fabulous. It must have fifteen rooms, although Chris only uses a few of them. You and Brose should go tonight."

I could see Brose's mouth starting to open in refusal, so I said coaxingly, slipping my hand into his, "I've always been mad to see the inside of that house, haven't you, Brose? It's been closed up as long as I can remember."

"Yeah, but—" Brose began.

"And if everybody goes," I rushed on, as though I hadn't heard him, "it's sure to be lots of fun. I mean, even if we aren't interested in art, or Chris Claypool, it would be worth going just to see the Fletcher house. Hawk's Rest," I murmured dreamily. "Doesn't it sound intriguing?"

"Well, yeah," Brose agreed grudgingly. "It'd be kind of interesting to get into the house. But Claypool—"

"Oh, you won't have to see much of him," Kay backed me up, grasping my plan of strategy with true feminine intuition. "And it would be silly to pass up a chance to see the Fletcher place just because Chris happens to own it now."

"He'll probably be so busy with all that crowd around," I said casually, "he'll hardly notice we're there."

"Brother!" Itchy wagged his head admiringly. "What teamwork! You girls ought to be on the football squad, the way you run interference for each other." He turned to grin at Brose. "It'd be a shame to waste all this psychology they're using on us, wouldn't it? Shall we be big and take 'em to Claypool's shindig tonight?"

"I guess so," Brose consented, grining back at Itchy with utterly infuriating male superiority.

19

Art for art's sake

A WAVE OF VOICES AND LAUGHTER MET us as we approached the Fletcher house that night. And no sooner were we inside than I began seeing people I knew. Kay hadn't exaggerated. Simply everyone was there. It was all very gay and Bohemian and informal. People perched on the arms of chairs and couches, or sat on the floor, or stood about looking at the mad collection of Chris's paintings ranged around the walls. Others rambled curiously through the house, as we proceeded to do.

The big, old-fashioned rooms opened one out of another, front parlor, back parlor, dining room. The furniture was elegant and Victorian, time faded, some pieces still shrouded in white dust covers. A round table was covered with a rather bizarre assortment of food, all kinds of fancy cheeses, plates of crackers and cookies, a great cut-glass punchbowl filled with an orangey-looking concoction, a silver urn of coffee. The urn needed polishing badly, but nobody minded. Everybody helped himself to whatever appealed to him, and then walked around eating or drinking it. A large ornate phonograph in one corner of the thronged back parlor was emitting the somewhat raucous strains of Shostakovich. And in the front parlor, someone was pounding out boogie on a square rosewood piano, sadly in need of tuning. It was astonishing how well the two widely divergent tunes went together. Or maybe it was just that the din of talk and laughter was so loud, you couldn't hear the discords.

"What a brawl!" Brose said.

I nodded. But, inwardly, I found myself quite intrigued. This was unlike any party I had ever attended. The setting was so unusual, the whole atmosphere excitingly sophisticated. Looking around at familiar faces, I wondered if it was Chris's influence that made the crowd seem fascinating and strange, or whether the curious background lent them an unaccustomed glamour. All of us seemed older, more worldly somehow, sitting around nibbling exotic cheeses, trying to discuss Picasso and Dali with some degree of intelligence, or simply clustering in awed knots before Chris's unconventional paintings.

Chris himself was nowhere about, although I looked for him surreptitiously as we moved from one room to another.

"Fine host!" Brose hissed to Itchy. "Doesn't even mingle with his guests."

"Oh, he'll turn up eventually. He always does. He's probably showing some palpitating female the moon from the terrace." The smile Itchy gave Brose was more like a leer.

"He'd better not try showing you any moon," Brose informed me belligerently.

"I've already seen it," I soothed, tucking my hand through the crook of his elbow.

Eventually Brose unbent a little and began to enjoy

himself. And even after Chris put in an appearance and started drifting amiably from one group to another, Brose behaved very well, although I felt his arm stiffen as Chris came up and laid a welcoming hand on each of our shoulders.

"If it isn't my lovely model and her friend," Chris greeted us pleasantly.

After a few minutes of casual conversation, he moved on and I felt Brose relax, his expression slightly sheepish. Personally, I was a little disappointed.

Later, strolling home through the moonlight, Brose said, "He didn't seem too objectionable tonight. But I still think his ideas about art are screwy."

I felt a small nip of resentment at this attitude. "You don't suppose it's barely possible he knows a little more about it than you?" I couldn't resist asking.

"Well, sure," Brose agreed magnanimously. "At least, he should if he's been earning a living as a commercial artist. The kind of pictures they use in advertising make sense."

"Kay told me," I informed Brose, "that commercial art stifles Chris. That's why he's broken free of it this summer to express himself, to paint as he feels."

"He must not feel very well then," Brose stated flatly. . . .

I happened to wake up quite early the following morning. And, moved by a sudden impulse, I got into my bathing suit and a terry-cloth beach skirt quietly, without disturbing anyone. I had a bite of breakfast in the kitchen, then tiptoed around, gathering up the paints Alicia had loaned me and a sketch pad she'd left.

Maybe the fine warm glow I felt was inspiration, I told

myself, as I slipped out into the freshness of early morning. The sun was just clearing the trees to the east and the sky was a mixture of palest blue and little fleecy pink clouds. The air smelled good and a wonderful stillness lay over everything. It was as if I had the whole world to myself.

I made my way briskly down to the beach, restraining an impulse to sing with the newly awakening birds. The yellow stretch of sand was deserted and gentle little waves broke on it with a flirt of foam, like white lace petticoat ruffles. They tempted me to swim, but first I meant to try my hand at painting. This should be a good time for my initial attempt, with no one around to see or disparage. I dipped up some lake water in the glass I had brought along, set it firmly in the damp sand and dropped down, cross-legged, Alicia's sketch pad on my knees.

I don't know how long I sat there, mixing water colors and dabbing them on happily. Lots of bluish green squiggles, that was the lake. A splash of dramatic dark green, representing Gull Island with its jagged crown of trees. The trouble was, I decided squinting through my eyelashes, as I'd seen Kay Lamb do when she was hard at work, this had too much reality. It was possible, almost, to recognize Gull Island and the lake, which was not the way modern painting was supposed to turn out. I mixed up some blackish green and dabbed it here and there, next I applied pink and yellow generously to represent the sky. But the whole thing, I decided, frowning, now looked like nothing so much as one of those slightly grotesque efforts turned out by kindergarten pupils.

A voice spoke at my shoulder and I was so startled I dropped my paintbrush. It went slithering across the sketch pad, leaving a wavering yellow streak in its wake.

Chris Claypool chuckled, "That helped a little—but

not much." He went on then, picking up my brush and wiping the sand from it onto his loudly patterned trunks, "The thing is, you haven't quite got the feel of it yet, haven't learned to let your imagination free. You're imprisoned in form and your colors are too close to reality."

I nodded, listening raptly as he talked, watching as he dipped the paintbrush into one unexpected color after another and splashed lines and circles and all sorts of lopsided blobs across my painting. It looked much less like the lake and Gull Island when he was finished, but the effect was certainly more original and striking than my efforts had been.

"Come on," Chris said, grabbing my hand and pulling me unceremoniously to my feet. "Let's have a swim before the lake gets all cluttered up. This is the best time of day."

"I know," I said, slipping out of my beach shirt and racing with him toward the water.

We splashed in and the icy chill made me clench my teeth hard for a minute. But once we were wet it was wonderful. Chris was a powerful swimmer, but he cut his speed to mine. We swam far out beyond the raft, then paralleled the shore for a way. Chris waved and pointed and of one accord we headed toward his little beach.

Laughing and breathless, we dropped down on the sand. Sunshine poured over our backs like warm molasses. We lay there, talking, as the sun climbed higher. Some of our conversation was about art, but not all of it. Chris told me a lot about himself and his work with a big Chicago advertising agency. And I found myself talking to him as freely as if we were old friends. Despite his being older and so very attractive, he was as easy to be with as any of the boys I'd known for ages. And much more interesting.

When I finally said I'd have to be getting home, Chris swam part way back to the main beach with me, then turned and cut away through the water with a friendly wave. As I reached the beach and walked up out of the water, unbuckling my bathing cap and shaking out my hair, I saw Brose crossing the sand toward me. It was still so early that only a few other swimmers were around, along with a crowd of sun-suited small fry playing in the sand.

"Hi," Brose hailed me cheerfully. "I see you beat me down this morning. Your folks didn't know where you'd gone."

"I've been up since six," I said. "Look, I even painted a picture before I went for a swim."

I picked up the sketch pad, where it lay with my paint-box and beach shirt, and showed it to Brose. With a complete lack of appreciation, he burst out laughing. I should have known better than to expect a more intelligent reaction from him.

Kay and Itchy joined us then and Kay took the pad from me and studied it solemnly. "Why Tobey!" she exclaimed, staring at me in surprise. "This is wonderful!"

"It is?" Itchy cracked. "I mean, it is!"

"I didn't do it all myself," I explained to Kay, ignoring Brose and Itchy. "Chris helped me quite a bit."

The amusement faded from Brose's face as though an eraser had passed across it. "Chris helped you?" he repeated, looking around as though he half expected to see him hiding in the shrubbery that fringed the beach. "Where is he now?"

"Oh, he's gone home," I said airily. "We went for a nice long swim, all the way up to his beach. In fact," I added, spreading out my beach shirt and dropping down on it, "I've had just about enough swimming for one morning. But I'll wait here for the rest of you, if you like."

I buried my face on my crossed arms, but out of one corner of my eye, I could see Brose's muscular legs standing there, indecisive, for a minute. Then he joined Kay and Itchy. But he was back long before they came in from the diving raft.

"Tobey," he said, dropping down beside me, "why didn't you whistle for me when you came down early?"

"I didn't want to wake everybody," I explained. "Besides, I meant to try painting and I know how utterly humorous you find that."

"Aw, gee, Tobey." Brose laid his hand over mine. "I don't mean to make you mad, but this modern art is so loopy."

"You think that," I informed him, "because you don't understand it."

"And I suppose you do," Brose said, "now that Claypool's explained it all to you."

"Well, I know more about it than I did," I admitted. "Chris is a wonderful teacher."

"I'll bet!" Brose scowled. "I noticed you didn't spend much time painting. You went swimming, too."

"Well, yes," I said in as dreamy a tone as possible. I'd get even with him for making light of my picture.

"Tobey," Brose coaxed, "don't go getting silly over this crack-pot artist like the rest of the dopey dames around here. You've got more sense—I hope."

"Have I?" I sighed.

Brose demanded, his frown deepening, "Are you actually going to waste your time like this, after all the things we planned to do, the fun we figured on having?"

"Oh, it needn't spoil our fun," I assured him. "I won't

paint all the time. But Chris makes it seem so fascinating, I just have to try my hand at it a little. Why don't you, too?"

"Me?" Brose rasped. "Do I look like I'm crazy?"

His glare was so menacing, I didn't dare needle him any further.

20

Chris has an idea

NEVER HAD A VACATION BEEN MORE fun. The days were full and running over with all the usual activities. Brose and I swam and played tennis, danced to the club juke box, went canoeing or on moonlight beach picnics with the crowd. And besides all this there was art, under the informal supervision of Chris Claypool.

Could his interest in me be merely because he claimed to find my work promising? I wasn't quite sure. And this uncertainty lent a definite spark to our relationship. It made me wonder if his hand didn't linger on my shoulder longer than was necessary when he showed me how to improve my painting. It made me thrillingly aware that he spent more time with me than he seemed to with any of the other amateur artists. I might have felt this was sheer wishful thinking on my part, but Kay insisted he was obviously attracted to me.

"It's just terribly exciting," Kay said earnestly. "The sort of burning way he looks at you, the way he hangs around, even with Brose doing all he can to discourage him. I mean it would simply give me goose bumps if Chris showed half as much interest in me—" her voice quavered off in a sigh.

"Oh, you're exaggerating," I said, hoping she wasn't.

There was enchantment in the thought of a smooth older man, one as popular as Chris, liking me best. *If* he did. But if he didn't, why did he waste so much time on me?

Brose was forever griping about it. "What's he always hanging around for?" he demanded. "Why doesn't he go and paint? He's in my hair day and night. I never get you to myself any more."

"You've got me to yourself right now, haven't you?" I asked reasonably. We were out on the raft at the moment, with only water around us.

"Yeah, but he'll probably swim up any minute," Brose growled, "showing off that crawl of his trying to horn in."

I teased, "There just seems to be something about the atmosphere here at Green Lake, that doesn't encourage twosomes. Look at the way Kentucky Jackson haunted us last year."

Brose glared at me ferociously. "Of all the ancient history to bring up! I thought you got over that."

"Oh, I did," I assured him sweetly. "So why can't you put up with Chris paying a little attention to me?"

We didn't actually quarrel, in the sense of completely losing our tempers with each other. But things were by no means smooth between us. We needled each other a lot and even when we'd be out walking, or driving around on a wonderful moonlit night, our kisses were more like brief armed truces than real expressions of affection. And yet I didn't like Brose any less than before. It was just that Chris's attentions were so flattering, I couldn't do anything very drastic to stop them. Sometimes, even when

Brose would be holding my hand, I'd find myself remembering something Chris had said, seeing again the quizzical way his eyebrows often tilted over his bright blue eyes, giving him a devilish look.

I worked on Brose to get him to try painting, but he wouldn't. Itchy fooled around with it a little, as did some of the other boys. But Brose would have no part of it. He took his resentment out on me by going on day-long fishing expeditions with his father and mine. But this only left me more time to spend with Chris, so he gave that up rather quickly.

Dad was just as glad. He confided to me, a little twinkle in his eye, "Brose gets fidgety after about an hour and starts thrashing around and peering toward shore to see if he can spot you. Why are you making life so miserable for him this summer?"

"I don't know," I admitted, moved by an urge to be quite honest with my father. "It's—as if I can't help myself, as if something just drives me to torment him."

Dad shook his head. "You must be growing up," he said in a half-dubious tone. "Not that I'm any authority," he added. "But, after all, as the father of four daughters, I'd be pretty stupid if I hadn't picked up a few facts about female psychology. When females are children," he went on to explain, "they treat males as friends and equals. But as they approach young maturity, I have noted this irresistible urge they seem to develop, this need to tease and torment their male admirers, to make their lives miserable. Your sister Janet went through it and so did Alicia. Remember how she used to treat Adam?"

I nodded thoughtfully. "And yet she loved him. They seem to be very happy now that they're married."

"Oh, to be sure," Dad said. "Love has nothing to do

with this urge. Or maybe it does, at that. Maybe it's the men they care for that girls are the hardest on." He studied me speculatively.

I felt color creep across my face. "You mean—maybe it's because I'm in love with Brose that I'm being so rough on him?"

"Far be it from me," Dad said firmly, "to try to implant any such idea in your head. I wasn't discussing you two exclusively. I was talking about all girls and all boys and the strange universal laws that seem to govern their behavior toward each other. Let's close the subject on that plane, shall we?"

Just the same, I couldn't help thinking afterwards about what Dad had said. I decided to feel Mom out on the question.

That evening as I was peeling potatoes and she was flouring the bass Dad had caught and preparing it for frying, I asked her, "Did you ever feel, 'way back before you and Dad were married, like treating him real mean for no special reason?"

Mom stared at me a little blankly for a minute, then a slow smile curled her mouth. "Now that's a strange thing to ask."

"Yes, but did you?" I pressed.

Mom's smile widened and she nodded. Her voice dipped conspiratorially. "There were times," she admitted, "when I treated him fiendishly. Why he ever asked me to marry him, I don't know."

I stared at her. Mom and Dad got along as well or better than the parents of anyone I knew. I just couldn't imagine her picking on him. "Why?" I asked wonderingly.

Mom's shoulders moved in a tiny shrug. "Who knows? It just seems to be the nature of women sometimes to be difficult. It's as if—" her amused glance lifted from the fish she was readying for the pan, "well, maybe it's a little like fishing, Tobey. You know how a fish will put up a terrific battle so it won't be caught? Maybe we're like that, too. When we realize we're really fond of a man—well, it's as if some instinct drives us to fight hard against it, even to the extent of making him miserable."

I nodded slowly. It wasn't exactly a glamorous simile, but I saw what she meant. I saw quite clearly. . . .

Chris came up to Kay and me on the beach the next morning with his usual warm greeting. Both of us were busy painting and he made some helpful suggestions. But he stood beside me, I noticed, instead of Kay. And his hand lingered on mine as he took my brush in order to add a touch of bright yellow to one corner of my painting, for contrast. It was a good thing, I thought, that Brose had driven into town with Itchy to buy some groceries for their mothers. He'd have been furious over Chris's actions.

"You know what I've been thinking?" Chris asked.

Kay and I shook our heads.

"We should have an amateur art show," Chris suggested with great enthusiasm, "to wind up the summer properly. So many people have been painting, we could have quite a display."

"Oh, Chris!" Kay exclaimed. "What a swell idea!"

"I think so, too," I agreed with equal fervor.

Chris nodded, apparently warming more and more to his scheme. "We can have it at my place," he decided, "next Sunday. A couple of artist friends of mine are coming out to help me pack and get ready to get back to town. They can be the judges."

Kay looked suddenly desolate and I'm sure my expression matched hers. It was the first we had heard of Chris's intention to leave so soon. The thought of not seeing him every day was a sharp hurt inside of me, followed by an even bigger pain at the realization that I might never see him again once he left the lake. But I tried to comfort myself with the reflection that Chicago wasn't so very far from Edgewood. Maybe he'd drive out to see me once in a while, at least until I left for college. . . . By the time I roused from my rosy daydream and got back to the present, Kay and Chris were deep in a discussion of plans for the art show.

Chris was saying, "Of course, neither Hilary nor Rufe will know a soul around here. But just to avoid the slightest suspicion of favoritism, we'll simply identify each painting by a number until after the final judging."

"That would be perfectly fair," I nodded.

And Kay agreed, "Oh, yes. And so exciting and mysterious, too. No one would know who painted which picture until the winner had been picked."

"Except me, of course," Chris chuckled. "And I won't tell."

We couldn't wait to spread the news about the art show. And practically everyone thought it was a terrific idea. Such artistic activity as went on the next few days, you couldn't even imagine! It was impossible to go anywhere without stumbling over an earnest amateur artist, hard at work on what she or he hoped would turn out to be a masterpiece. I worked hard myself on a scene back of our cottage, which I felt was rather unusual.

"Creeps sake!" Brose exploded, the third time he dropped over and found me painting. "What a way to spend a vacation!"

"I'm enjoying it," I said serenely.

He stood there, glowering down at my sketch pad. "Is

that post-impressionist or surrealist?" he asked, using some of the words he'd picked up from Chris, but with an utterly sarcastic inflection. "It sure doesn't look like much of anything to me."

"Why don't you paint something, if you can do better?"

Brose kicked at a stone on the ground. "I've got more amusing ways to waste my time!" he snapped. "I'll be glad when the darned old art show's over and Claypool goes home."

"Will you?" I asked, my tone implying that I wouldn't.

Brose laid a coaxing hand on my arm. "Skip it and let's go out in the canoe."

I shook my head. "I can't now. I have to finish this and get it over to Chris's. After all, the show's tomorrow."

Brose said sarcastically, "Gee, I can hardly wait!"

I ignored that. "I'll go swimming with you around four if you like, after Kay and I take our paintings over."

"Well, okay," Brose said, "if you're sure you can spare the time." He gave me a sour look and stalked off.

When Kay and I took our paintings up to Hawk's Rest, Chris numbered them and put them with a stack of other entries.

"We've got over fifty pictures," he said jubilantly. "More than I expected."

Kay asked, "Haven't your artist friends come yet?" I knew she had been looking forward to meeting two new men.

Chris shook his head. "They're driving up tomorrow."

He invited us out onto the terrace and the three of us sat there for quite a while, drinking Cokes and talking. The water stretched blue and clear beyond a fringe of tall old trees.

"I'll miss all this," Chris said, a note of nostalgia in his voice. "It's been a wonderful summer. Rest, relaxation, a complete change from the rat race of trying to satisfy a bunch of high-pressure advertising clients. And I've had a chance to think out some things that were bothering me, too."

He seemed to be talking more to himself than to us, but Kay and I hung interestedly on his words.

When he paused to light a cigarette, I asked sympathetically, "Will you hate it awfully, getting back to work for that agency?"

"If I get a high enough price for Hawk's Rest," Chris told us, "maybe I'll chuck my job and try illustrating."

"You mean you've got a buyer?" Kay asked.

"Well, at least a good solid nibble," Chris chuckled. "A man wants to turn it into a resort hotel. Says it has atmosphere. Can't you just imagine what Uncle Jeremiah would say to that? But who can afford to keep up a place like this nowadays? I hope the deal will finance a good long trip to Mexico."

I drifted off into a bright dream of getting fascinating letters postmarked "Mexico." But the sound of the doorbell jarred me out of it. Some more people had arrived with paintings for the show. Kay and I were astounded to notice that most of the afternoon had slipped away. We told Chris good-bye rather hastily, since Kay had promised to go swimming with Itchy at the same time I had agreed to meet Brose. And we were already quite late.

We rushed home and into our bathing suits, then practically ran down to the beach together.

"They'll be perfectly furious," Kay said. "Probably they'll have taken up with some other women."

I suspected she was right. But we found them lying on the sand in what appeared to be exceptionally good spirits.

And, contrary to our fearful expectations, there were no girls with them, only the Williams' collie dog, Taffy, lying stretched out, wet and companionable, between them.

21

The art show

RATHER TO MY SURPRISE, BROSE DIDN'T object to attending the art show. Moreover, he called for me on time, properly dressed for the occasion and in a most amiable mood. This in itself should have aroused my suspicions. But it didn't. I simply thought that since Chris would be leaving so soon, Brose had decided to be magnanimous.

We strolled along the path toward Hawk's Rest hand in hand. It was dusk and the lake had a soft opalescent glow in the dimness. Fireflies twinkled here and there, like runaway stars.

Brose said, "I guess this show will be Claypool's swan song around here."

"I suppose you could look at it that way," I agreed.

"After tonight," Brose said, swinging my hand, "we can forget about him."

I didn't say anything, which Brose seemed to take for agreement.

He asked, evincing rather more interest than I had expected, "Will Claypool judge the pictures himself?"

"Oh, no," I told him. "A couple of artist friends of his from Chicago will do that."

Brose nodded. "That should be fair enough. Not that there's much at stake," he added. "Only ribbons."

"I'd be very proud to win a blue ribbon," I told him. "Or even a second or third award. Not that there's much chance."

"Why not?" Brose asked staunchly. "You've got as good a chance as anybody." He had to spoil it then by adding, "It's all such screwball stuff."

I didn't bother to answer. We were mounting the steps of Chris's house by that time and I didn't want to start an argument.

The big double parlors were thronged with people. Paintings were ranged around all the walls, each with its identifying number. Some of the pictures were conventional, most of them modern, indicating how strong was Chris's influence.

Brose followed me around, looking pained, as I admired and exclaimed over various entries. Finally he exploded, "Craziest stuff I ever saw! Why should otherwise normal people suddenly imagine they're artists?"

"It's a wonderful hobby," I pointed out. "Look at Winston Churchill—he paints for amusement and relaxation. So do lots of other famous people. And Grandma Moses—why, she's made a career of it and she didn't start till she was around seventy and couldn't see to embroider any more. That was why she took up art.

Brose grinned. "It you'd waited till you were that old, I could have stood it better."

Just then I felt a friendly hand on my shoulder and saw Brose stiffen. Chris greeted us both and I answered, smiling warmly. Brose muttered, "Hello," through his teeth.

There were two people with Chris. One was a short, pleasantly ugly young man in a coat and trousers that didn't match and a slightly crooked bow tie. The other was a stunning girl with the blackest hair and the bluest eyes I had ever seen combined. Her figure, in a white knitted dress, was spectacular.

"Hilary," Chris said, fondling the hand she had tucked possessively through his arm, "this is Tobey Heydon and Brose Gilman. Hilary Richards," he said and then, indicating the nice, mismatched individual, "and Rufe Edwards."

If I had ever been taken more completely by surprise, I couldn't think when! I had been so positive that both the friends Chris had spoken of were men. Hilary was one of those absolutely foul names that could belong to either sex.

And now this devastating creature was greeting Brose and me politely, then turning her full attention back to Chris, who was obviously basking in it. Rufe Edwards spoke to us, too, and I must have mumbled something not too fantastic, although I hadn't the faintest idea what I said. After a moment, Chris took his guests on to meet another group.

"Maybe," Brose said into my ear, "I should take a few art lessons myself. Do you suppose she'd teach me?"

I gave him a chill look, but he didn't see it. His glance was following Hilary Richards. "She's hanging onto Claypool as if he's her private property. Funny," Brose added, "but I got the impression from you that both his friends were men."

"Did you?" I asked, with an attempt at airy laughter.

Brose stared down at me, his glance going deep in a way

I didn't relish too much at the moment. He said, his voice a note lower, "You thought she was a man, too, didn't you?"

I shrugged. "It really doesn't matter. With a name like that, anyone can make a mistake."

Brose's fingers closed around mine.

I cringed a little inwardly at the sound of Hilary's entranced voice, exclaiming to Chris, "Darling, you mean it? You may get enough out of this mausoleum to finance our honeymoon in Mexico? How divine!"

Brose heard, too, but he didn't say anything. He just squeezed my hand a little harder.

Kay and Itchy charged up then and Kay demanded, "Aren't you devastated? I couldn't believe my eyes when I saw her."

"Neither could I," Itchy said wickedly.

The four of us stood there, talking for a while, then Brose said, "Well, let's look at the rest of the pictures."

"Have you seen Number Twenty-two?" Kay asked.

We hadn't, so she and Itchy led us over to the wall of the back parlor where it was hanging.

"Isn't it fabulous?" Kay exclaimed. "Everyone's simply dying to know who painted it. Some of them think it's Chris's work, that he just hung it with the others for a gag. It's so professional looking."

I stood there, staring at a painting all in varying shades of green, done in the airiest, lightest brush strokes you could imagine. There was an almost feathery texture about it that was indescribable, but that gave an effect of softness and lightness that was most unusual.

"This is good?" Brose asked unappreciatively.

"At least, it's different," Itchy admitted.

Kay and I exchanged pitying glances. Just a pair of low brows, that was what Brose and Itchy were when it came to art. Personally, I couldn't imagine who, among the amateurs at Green Lake, was capable of such superior work. As we moved on past painting after painting, I saw nothing to compare with it.

Soon Chris rapped on the piano for quiet in order to make the announcement everyone was waiting for. Hilary Richards hovered close beside him and he seemed very pleased with her nearness. Seeing them together, I felt a nip of resentment at Chris for not telling me about Hilary. But that was absurd, I reminded myself. The silly dream-world I had built up around him was no one's doing but my own—and I should have had more sense.

Chris wasted no time on preliminaries. He announced that the first prize had been awarded to Number Twenty-two.

A prolonged roar of applause followed. Apparently everyone had been impressed with the superior quality of that entry. I was rather annoyed with Brose for just standing there with a blank look on his face, not clapping or anything. Even when I nudged him, he didn't seem to notice.

A second later I learned the reason for his actions.

"Number Twenty-two," Chris said, and it seemed to me he was a little surprised at his own words, "is the work of Brose Gilman, who shows an amazing aptitude for art, new as he is at it."

Chris said quite a bit more, all very complimentary. Then he handed Brose the blue ribbon and shook his hand in hearty congratulation. I could only stare in astonishment, still unable to believe what was happening. Kay looked as surprised as I, but Itchy didn't.

"You knew Brose submitted it?" I asked Itchy.

He nodded, flushing. I couldn't imagine why he and Brose both seemed so embarrassed.

The other two awards were announced then and I didn't win either of them. But I didn't really care. I was too thrilled and impressed with Brose's success. People came crowding around us, all eager to congratulate Brose and rave over the excellence of his painting. Brose took his sudden acclaim with almost agonized modesty, which made me feel even more proud of him.

Chris and his two friends made their way back through the crowd to speak to Brose.

Hilary Richards admitted admiringly, "One doesn't often see such superior brushwork in an amateur's painting, Mr. Gilman. As one artist to another," she smiled at him warmly, "may I ask how you achieved that airy, feathery effect?"

Itchy emitted a queer choking sound. Kay and I frowned at him reprovingly, then looked back at Brose, for whose reply everyone waited expectantly.

Brose gulped, blushing, "Do you really want me to tell you how I did it?"

"Of course," Chris assured him.

Hilary and Rufe nodded.

Into the silence, Brose muttered, "Well—I kind of borrowed the Williams' dog and dipped his tail into this green paint I'd mixed up and then I got him to wag his tail against the paper. Several different shades of green I used and then Itchy'd pat Taffy's head and the dog would wag the paint onto the picture and—well—that's how I did it."

If possible the room was even more quiet than before. Everyone just stared at Brose. And then someone, Rufe

Edwards it turned out to be, began to laugh. Great, booming laughter in which, after a startled moment, everyone joined. I couldn't help howling myself at the picture summoned up by Brose's halting words. And I remembered him and Itchy the previous afternoon, lying so innocently on the beach with Taffy all wet between them. They had probably just finished washing the paint off of the dog when Kay and I joined them.

"Funniest thing I ever heard of," Rufe Edwards gasped when he could speak. He laid one hand on Chris's shoulder and one on Hilary's. "I guess we're not the only judges who've been kidded, though. Remember that exhibit where they had the winning picture hung upside down? And that other one where the award went to a canvas the artist had cleaned his paint brushes on?"

Brose assured them earnestly, "If you don't think it's fair, you can give the award to someone else. I know I'm no artist."

"I should say not," Rufe grinned at Brose.

And Hilary Richards shook her lovely head firmly in the negative.

Chris voiced the opinion of them all when he said, "In art, it's results that count, not methods."

So Brose kept his blue ribbon. Or, at least, he kept it until we were on our way home. Then he told me, "Here, Tobey, you take the darn' thing. I feel kind of funny about it all."

"Why?" I asked, but I let him press the ribbon into my hand. Knowing Brose, he'd probably lose it in a week if I didn't take it.

He admitted sheepishly, "I never figured the silly painting would win. I was burned up at you, going all out for art and Claypool. I just wanted to have an entry in the show so you'd realize anybody could paint that crazy way if he took a notion, that Chris wasn't such a big wheel."

"And now you're a big wheel yourself," I teased.

"Quit it," Brose said. "When it comes to art—"

But I didn't let him finish. "I find I am getting a little bored with art," I told him, curling my fingers in his as we walked slowly along.

"Well, good," Brose said fervently. "Let's forget it, shall we?"

I nodded.

"And Claypool—" Brose's tone was anxious, "can we forget him, too?"

"Hilary might get jealous if I don't," I said.

I could picture the two of them in Mexico on their honeymoon with scarcely a qualm now. I guessed I'd been pretty foolish, letting myself get so dazzled with Chris. Some time, if I kept on going off on silly tangents like that, Brose might not be around for me to come back to when I regained my senses. It was an appalling thought. I clung to his hand a little harder.

"I guess," I admitted, wanting to be completely honest about it, "Chris was just a crazy phase I went through. Thanks for waiting for me."

Brose's arms went around me, warm and strong. The moon made a glittering silver path across the water.

He said, his voice low, "I'll always wait for you, Tobey. You know that. But the summer's running out on us."

I nodded. "We won't waste another minute of it."

As our lips met, I felt my heart quicken. This was the way it should always be with us, understanding wrapping us about, no shadow of disagreement between us. This was one of those wonderful, special moments, when I wished I could stretch time out, making it last forever.